WINDS AND STRINGS AND SILVER WINGS

- Frank's Sonata -

FRANK BALENSIEFER

Bloomington, IN  Milton Keynes, UK

authorHOUSE

AuthorHouse™
1663 Liberty Drive,
Suite 200
Bloomington, IN 47403
www.authorhouse.com
Phone: 1-800-839-8640

AuthorHouse™ UK Ltd.
500 Avebury Boulevard
Central Milton Keynes, MK9 2BE
www.authorhouse.co.uk
Phone: 08001974150

This book is a work of non-fiction. Unless otherwise noted, the author and the publisher make no explicit guarantees as to the accuracy of the information contained in this book and in some cases, names of people and places have been altered to protect their privacy.

First published by AuthorHouse 4/27/2006

ISBN: 1-4259-0731-8 (sc)

Printed in the United States of America
Bloomington, Indiana

This book is printed on acid-free paper.

To my wife, Spunky Annie,
who puts the wind in my sails
and the song in my heart.

CONTENTS

PART III THE GOOD LIFE

PART I

WHEN YOU AND I
WERE YOUNG

GIVE ME THE SIMPLE LIFE

The Days Gone By

O the days gone by! O the days gone by!
The apples in the orchard, and the pathway through the rye;
The chirrup of the robin, and the whistle of the quail
As he piped across the meadows sweet as any nightingale;
When the bloom was on the clover, and the blue was in the
  sky,
And my happy heart brimmed over, in the days gone by.

In the days gone by, when my naked feet were tripped
By the honeysuckle tangles where in the water-lilies dipped,
And the ripples of the river lipped the moss along the brink
Where the placid-eyed and lazy-footed cattle came to drink,
And the tilting snipe stood fearless of the truant's wayward
  cry
And the splashing of the swimmer, in the days gone by.

O the days gone by! O the days gone by!
The music of the laughing lip, the luster of the eye;
The childish faith in fairies, and Aladdin's magic ring-
The simple, soul-reposing, glad belief in everything,
When life was like a story, holding neither sob nor sigh,
In the golden olden glory of the days gone by.

James Whitcomb Riley

These words depicted the essence of a boy's life in rural Indiana; mine was somewhat like that, although I must confess that much of my youth was spent in a small town. My happiest memories, however, are of times in the country.

In "real" times, we lived on a small farm for no more than two years, but memories of days and nights at my uncle's 160-acre farm eclipse reality. To this day I refer to "the farm" with nostalgic pleasure, as if I had spent my entire youth there. An appropriate adage that my mother often used was, "If wishes were horses, we'd all take a ride." And how I wished! But, I *did* ride.

The horses on the farm were gargantuan work horses, but to my cousin Connie (Conrad) and me, they were the Lone Ranger's "Silver" or Tom Mix' "Tony." It took considerable effort, but we somehow managed to mount up despite the beast's enormous height. As I recall, one of us would position the horse parallel to a high fence while the other would climb the fence and mount the bareback horse. Considering our abbreviated height (we were both nine years old) and the breadth of the huge horse, the mounting effort required doing the splits—painful, but the thrill was worth it.

One day, Connie and I both managed to climb aboard "Old Ted"— bareback of course, but on this day we used a real halter instead of just holding onto its mane, as we usually did. What a sight we created.

Astride Old Ted, our stiffened legs must have looked like splayed-out and broken clothespins.

"Smooth" is not an adjective you'd use to describe a ride on a plow-horse. It was more like riding a springless vehicle with square wheels. But we didn't mind. We were tough old cowboys out on the range. Unfortunately, Old Ted had a mind of his own, he decided to head for home. This required a sharp turn, for which we both were unprepared. The reins were of no help, so I dropped them and grabbed his mane. Connie grabbed me, and the mane seared my hands as we went flying down to the gravel road far below. We were battered, scraped and bruised, but suffered no broken bones. The horse trotted to the barn, obviously happy to be rid of his irksome burden. "You hurt?" Connie asked. "Not only hurt, but *mad*!" I fumed. "That dumb horse! He's supposed to stop and whinny and nuzzle you. I saw Tony do that to Tom Mix once."

Luckily, we weren't too far from the house, so under considerable pain, we limped and dragged ourselves to the back door. When Aunt Ruby saw us she cried out, "Holy Mother! What happened to you?" We jointly blurted out our tale of woe while she ministered our cuts and bruises. As I recall, we may have even exaggerated our misery somewhat in order to gain maximum sympathy—Aunt Ruby's "sympathy" often translated into a large piece of her incredibly delicious chocolate cake with white icing. Sure enough, while applying bandages, she tenderly said, "I'll bet some chocolate cake and milk would help the healing." Connie smiled and winked at me.

We ignored Old Ted and rode sheep (with easy to grab long wool) for some time after that episode.

YESTERDAY, WHEN I WAS YOUNG

S ome incidents in our past are best forgotten, but it isn't always easy. A classic example of this was an event that occurred when I was about eight.

We were living in a very small country town at the time. It was so small, in fact, that the designations "town" and "country" were blurred. Most residents had some form of livestock—cows, horses, sheep, goats, chickens—whatever was productive. We had a cow named Gertrude. She and I were very close (what with my head being pressed against her flank and my pre-warmed hands milking her and feeding her each morning). We could afford but little feed, so I had to take old Gert out daily, before the school bus arrived. I carried a large hammer, an iron stake, and a long chain. Usually, the area bordering the nearby railroad track provided enough weeds and grass to keep the cow chewing until I took her to our little barn after school.

Having always had a vivid imagination, it was easy for me to fantasize. Gertrude became my swift and agile cow pony. I was Buck Jones, Hopalong Cassidy, or John Wayne. I had made a gun holster out of a discarded leather purse and carved a "gun" out of some scrap wood. And if there had been a train robbery, why, I would have just saddled up, grabbed my six gun and—and—aw shucks! Who was I kidding? What good's an old wooden gun, anyway? I needed something that I could at least use to go hunting. Then it hit me: I could make a bow and arrow! I knew of a tree with strong and flexible branches. Some cattail stems or bamboo shoots would make good arrows, and there was some strong cord in the barn. It was a cinch! In a flash, I was Geronimo!

It didn't take long to manufacture my new and oh-so-clever arsenal, but I had to do it on the sly, which wasn't easy. If anyone in our family found out about my hazardous endeavor, it would be back to my faux forty-five—for my own good, of course. They would have said, "You're too young for something so dangerous. You could hurt something or someone else." Right! And I could fall down the stairs and break a leg, too. But no one found me out, and Geronimo was soon on the prowl.

One of our neighbors, Mr. Johnson, had a flock of chickens in his yard. They were noisy, messy, and just plain dumb! Maybe these factors helped me to rationalize what I did.

It was a long, lazy summer evening. I had finished my chores and had gone to the barn; there was always plenty of work to do there, so no one was aware of it when I slipped away with my bow and arrow. Night was about to fall. On a distant hill the outline of hundreds of marauding savage warriors rose like a band of crazed wolves. Their war whoops and the thundering hooves of horses would petrify the most fearless of men. But Geronimo was beyond fearless. He stood his ground bravely, calmly putting arrow to bowstring. He knew that once he had killed the enemy's chief, the rest would not only scatter in disarray, but also, they would tell other tribes of the brave, cunning, and strong Geronimo.

With keen eye and incredible strength, he pulled the bowstring to its limit, waiting for just the right moment. There he was! The enemy chief himself, proudly astride his swift pinto, roaring toward Geronimo with incredible speed. The time was NOW! The arrow left the bow like a streak of lightening and pierced the heart of the—chicken? Oh no! I couldn't believe what I had done. I was only pretending. I didn't mean to kill the chicken—did I? Wait! Maybe it was still alive—and maybe Mr. Johnson didn't see what happened. With a prayer on my quivering lips, I dropped my bow and rushed to the floundering chicken. But in my broken heart, I knew it was too late. A few weak "clucks" and it was all over. Having never killed anything but flies, the experience made me sick. Compounding my distress was the thought of Mr. Johnson discovering what I had done. I hadn't just killed one chicken; its death meant no more eggs from it—no more little chicks. Good Lord, I'd wiped out a whole generation! What was I to do?

I don't recall my father ever giving us much advice or meting out many rules, but one thing he was *very* adamant about was honesty. If I were to associate any slogan with him, it would be, "Honesty is the best policy." Having been deeply imbued with this attribute, I knew that I would have no peace within until I had gone to Mr. Johnson, confessed my terrible murderous act, and taken my lumps.

There was little sleep for me that night. The clucking chickens across the road seemed to be saying, "Killer! Murderer!"

The next morning, I don't think Gertrude enjoyed the milking any more than I did. My hands were cold and trembling as I gave her a rush job. I *had* to see Mr. Johnson before the school bus arrived. I dashed across the road just as he was walking toward the flock of chickens. My throat was dry and my heart was pounding as I hesitatingly approached him. "Why Frank, you're pale as a ghost. What in the world is wrong?" he asked. Through parched lips, I said, "My dad told me to always be honest, Mr. Johnson, even if it hurts." Tears welled in my eyes as I added, "I—I killed one of your chickens with my bow and arrow last night. I'm really, really sorry, Mr. Johnson. What can I do to make up for it?" I didn't know how he would react, but it was nothing like I expected. He just gave a kind of half-smile, put his huge hand on my shoulder and said, "I know, boy, I know. You see, the missus and I happened to be looking over our flock when we saw you come across the road looking like an Indian on the warpath. When your arrow hit the chicken, we thought you were going to go into shock. We decided to see what you would do about it today. Your folks taught you right, boy, so you know there have to be some consequences. Tell you what—come around after school and I'll have a list of chores for you."

That was it. No chiding or tongue-lashing, just "work it off." What a relief! I thought, "Boy! Mr. Johnson's my kind of guy."

Ten years later I enlisted in what was then called the Army Air Corps, and, although we had moved to a town 25 miles from the Johnsons, they joined my family at the train depot to help "see me off." There were tears and cover-up laughter, as you might expect, since I was the first of the eligible boys in my family to enlist. As I was about to board the train, Mrs. Johnson, misty-eyed, handed me a box lunch, gave me a quick hug, then moved back quickly as I stepped to the platform.

The doleful train whistle blew as we pulled away and I was soon watching my family and friends fade into the distance. The wheels on the track seemed to be saying, "Click-clack, you can't go back. Clickity-clack, you can't go back." I was sad to leave my sheltered life, but excited to think of the strange and somewhat frightening new world I was about to enter. My thoughts soon were diverted to the box lunch by a mouth-watering aroma. I lifted the top with enthusiasm. A napkin covered the food. On the napkin was written in a sort of hen-scratched fashion, "Good hunting, Frank." Under the napkin was the source of the wonderful aroma—fried chicken! I smiled to myself as I thought, "Bless you, Mrs. J. You just made my day."

HOORAY FOR HOLLYWOOD

"**B**oyhood" should be a time of freedom. Freedom from worry, from heavy responsibility, from the weighty problems of the world. A time for exploration and growth. A time for—girls! More about warm and soft things later.

My brothers and I had a different kind of boyhood. Our younger, formative years were rather normal—for a poor family of 13 souls. Each of us can recall some happy moments, and I don't recall ever having to go to bed without an evening meal. But, when one of us boys turned 12, it was understood that we were to work in Dad's Mobil Oil filling station. We were required to do everything within our physical abilities. This included such functions as fixing flat tires, mounting wheels, greasing cars and changing oil—not to mention giving "full service" at the gasoline pump. True to his Germanic lineage, Dad was the original "Mr. Clean." His idea of full service was doing just about everything short of washing and waxing the happy customer's car. We filled the fuel tank (ever wonder why the gasoline dispenser is called a "pump?" We didn't, because that's exactly what we had to do). We washed *all* of the windows, checked the oil, the water, and other fluid levels, checked and filled the tires, and, on some occasions, even vacuumed the car!

I was the dreamer in the family. The pie-in-the-sky guy who envisioned a romantic life of ease. Pumping gas, greasing cars, and all the rest of it just didn't get it with me. I couldn't see life as a "grease monkey."

On a rare occasion, we were allowed to see a movie— for the bank-breaking cost of 25 cents. (Note: Since these memoirs will contain some true confessions, the first will be that I sneaked into the theater once and kept the quarter. I was absolved in the confessional, but have not forgotten the transgression). One of the movies that had an indirect effect on my future had a scene in which Mickey Rooney, who was wearing a tweed sports coat, slipped into an overcoat without first grasping the sports coat sleeve! I was amazed, because I had never seen an overcoat with such slick, satin lining in the arms. What elegance! What luxury! I also noticed that actors in California scenes very seldom wore outer coats. I inferred from this—and other clues—that California must indeed be a paradise.

The movie that provided a seminal moment in my life, however, was "The Prince and the Pauper," starring the Mauch twins. In my mind, I looked so much like them that I could have passed for their triplet brother. What a life they must have led. Fame, fortune, freedom. Why couldn't I share in the good life? Why *shouldn't* I? After all, I was pretty old for 12; I had the looks, the *savior faire*, the talent, the acting ability (school plays, y'know). Surely someone would "discover" me if I could but get to Hollywood.

We had maps at the filling station, so I reviewed a United States map and laid out plans for my great adventure. I would hitchhike and pick up odd jobs along the way. There would surely be gas pumps that needed tending all the way from Chicago to L.A. on Route 66. I reckoned that the pain of losing me to Hollywood would quickly be eased when the family became the beneficiaries of my largesse. A new car for Dad, a fur coat and new washing machine for Mom, clothes and gifts for my brothers and sisters. I was the little train that could. Trains—boxcars—there's a thought. I'd *do* it! Hollywood or Bust!

One of my sisters had a suitcase of sorts, so, confiding in no one, I somehow managed to get it and put it under the bed. Note that I didn't say "my bed" (I should be so lucky!). Having our own bed was but a dream—as was a house with more than one bath!

With so many siblings everywhere, packing was no mean feat. But there wasn't a lot that I had to pack anyway. Pants, a sweater, shirts, socks, etc. I had saved every penny of the tips I received from our surprised and happy customers, so I didn't leave home penni-less—yet, I knew that my meager earnings wouldn't last long.

When departure time came, it was a warm summer day and my plans were complete. Pick up the suitcase from the back of the tool shed on the way to the Mobil station (which was only a few blocks from home, but near the highway); make a right turn on highway 41 and start hitchhiking to Chicago. I didn't dare think about Mom—who would be in tears and saying her rosary as she read my note. I made it short and sweet; it went something like this:

Dear Mom, Dad, and all—

I know you'll think I'm crazy, but I have to prove myself as a successful actor. I promise to send as much money as possible as soon as possible. I know you'll be sad, Mom, and you'll be mad, Dad. My brothers will probably be envious and the girls will be worried. But you all know how I hate being stuck in this filling station rut.

I'm deeply sorry for the hurt this causes, but I'll make it up to you—just pray for me.

All My Love,
Frank

I left the note in the mailbox on the way out.

When I left home, there were actually only eight children left. One of my sisters, Leona, was in a convent and the second oldest, Millie, was a live-in housemaid about 150 miles north in an upscale Chicago suburb. My plan was to spend my first night with her, then hit Route 66 the next morning.

Filled with youthful confidence, I had no trouble in getting a ride all the way to Evanston. My guardian angel was a nice older fellow who listened to my story and took me right to Millie's doorstep. My profuse thanks brought only a combined smile and frown from the gentleman.

I always considered Millie to be broad-minded, caring, and understanding, so I was shocked and disappointed when she forcefully demanded that I return to my family in Fowler, Indiana. She pointed out something that I had overlooked. She first told me how lucky I had been to be picked up by such an honorable gentleman and just how horrible it *might* have been. But the clincher was her reminding me that since I was only a juvenile, the state troopers would undoubtedly "haul me in" and force me to either go home or become a ward of the state. That fact was the pin that popped my bubble.

Millie was kind but firm as she put me on the train to Fowler. She told me that she had called Dad and asked him to meet me at the train depot. The mere thought gave me a cold sweat. You had to know my father. Well, in truth, you couldn't really *know* him, you could just know *about* him. He was a hard study. I'm sure he loved us—his children—but he could neither say so nor show affection. Honor, duty, dauntless integrity, and *honesty* were characteristics everyone who knew him associated with him. We, his children, lived in fear of him, yet he rarely struck any of us. When angry, which was often, one withering look from him could make a Paul Bunyan tremble. He mentioned his boxing ring prowess many times, fine tuning our fear of him.

What troubled us most was the way he treated our mother, who was gentle as a lamb—and nearly as sacrificial. I honestly don't know about the physical abuse, but the vilifying, demeaning verbal abuse was enough to make us weep. And Mom didn't dare utter a word. She should be canonized, not only for living an exemplary life of faith, hope, and charity, but also for being a real martyr. May she rest in peace. I actually believe that he resented our mother for having so many children (go figure!). And he was jealous of us because Mom showed her affection for us so openly. He was a very frustrated, bitter, angry and confused man.

Try, then, to imagine the scenario I had envisioned as the train sped me to my dreaded encounter. Dad had never struck me—nor had he ever had such good reason to as I now provided.

As the train pulled into the station, my heart was pounding; my mouth was dry; my knees were weak—

and I wished I were dead. No only had I disappointed and frightened my parents, but also, Dad had to leave the Mobil station with my 15-year-old brother, Joe, to run it!

Then I saw them on the platform. Red-eyed Mom—wringing her hands. Red-faced Dad—grinding his teeth and clenching his fists. There was nothing I could do but pray for mercy.

When I slowly stepped off the train, Mom quickly enveloped me in her ample bosom—not unlike a mother hen, shielding its own. I wanted to look at Dad to see what he was going to do, but was afraid of what I'd see (I couldn't anyway—Mom had my head buried). Then I felt my arm being nearly crushed in a vise-like grip (I think Dad could bend a tire iron with his fingers), as he growled through gritted teeth, "You're *nuts*, boy—you know that?! Nuts!! Now get back to work!" All I could manage to mumble was, "Sorry, Dad." I was whipped, but he never laid a hand on me.

Part of the price I had to pay for my transgression was working under Dad's grudging, cold, and sullen temperament. And, although I was grateful that nothing worse had happened, when the triple-threat odor of petroleum—gasoline, oil, and grease—hit my nostrils, I was more determined than ever to live an entirely different life than the "work-only" one to which I had been chained.

My dream of an acting career was put on hold, but not entirely abandoned. High school days would come soon. Surely life would improve. Considering disappointment, however, in retrospect, I can see the benefit of Dad's strict discipline and of the tough times of my youth. They strengthened my resolve and helped me learn to cope with adversity.

Thanks, Dad. You knew best. Thanks, Mom. Your unfaltering love is still alive in each of us.

BAA BAA BLACK SHEEP

I suppose every family has at least one child who is more difficult to raise than the others. My parents were blessed with not one, but two. The eldest, Joe, led a profligate, dissolute life, yet died helping a neighbor. Were he alive today, he would readily—even proudly—agree with my non-judgmental observations about his life.

Joe was born to sin. He was the antithesis of all that Mom and Dad stood for. But nearly everyone loved him. He was charming, good-looking, witty—some would call him charismatic. He was the quintessential con man. He could sell an electric heater to a dying man in a Death Valley summer. Think I'm kidding? You should have seen a couple of cars he sold me. Yes, he dropped out of school and, later, became a car salesman. And was he good! If the car he was selling smoked like a winter chimney, he would pass it off as the result of someone having put a poor grade of fuel in it. "Just add an can of Rislone; it'll be okay. In fact, I happen to have a can you can have for half price!"

Joe was not schizophrenic, but he could be a Dr. Jekyl or a Mr. Hyde. He would have been a marvelous case study for Freud or Jung. When I think of Joe, I envision a broad, warm smile shielding white-hot raw anger. Many's the door or wall—or jaw—that felt his lightening-like fist. It was as though he were "possessed." He would go to taverns and itch for a fight. On the slightest provocation, he would knock someone flat with one punch. Fortunately, he never killed anyone. Fortunately, also, he found an outlet for this overwhelming need to explode—boxing. In those days, young men could compete in Golden Gloves boxing. Joe *loved* it. As you might expect, he never lost a fight. Of course, he needed a sparring partner. I was the honoree. I have a broken nose and a lot of painful memories as evidence.

It was sad, really. You couldn't stay mad at the guy once you knew of his inner turmoil. But what upset me most was to witness the anguish he caused Mom and Dad—not to mention his brothers and sisters. How often I saw tears in my mother's eyes as she fervently said her rosary, praying that Joe would come home—safe and sound—from having run away for the umpteenth time.

I can recall one night in particular with crystal clarity. It was late. Dad was at work, as usual. Mom was ironing clothes and praying for Joe's return. I can still hear the sizzle as her tears dropped to the hot iron. I don't know why I happened to be up at that hour, but as I was trying to console Mom, the back door quietly opened and Joe slipped in, looking furtively about to be sure Dad wasn't there. It's a wonder Mom didn't drop the iron. Her voice was laden with pathos as she cried, "Jesus, Mary and Joseph!" The remembrance of the embrace that followed still tears at my heart. The rest of the incident is mercifully blurred by the protective glaze of time gone by. But I do believe that Joe left rather quickly, having gathered some food and necessities.

My mother's love for each of her eleven children (there would have been twelve, but one died at birth) was unqualified and unquantified. She loved saint and sinner, whatever pain and suffering she had to endure. And suffer and sacrifice she did. Her fingers were continually cracked and bleeding. But she offered it up for the poor souls. She received her eternal reward while lying in bed, saying the rosary with Dad.

Joe would give you the shirt off his back. He gave more than that to his neighbor in Phoenix. He gave his life.

Joe was a swimming pool salesman so he knew something about pool equipment, pumps, filters, etc. One day he noticed that his neighbor was having trouble with his pool filter, so, in wet swim trunks only, he left his pool to offer help. I don't know all of the details, but I do know that he was electrocuted and died instantly. Though born to sin, he died through an act of charity. He was thirty-five.

BAA BAA BLACK SHEEP II

A n eerie thing happened as Joe's body lay in an open casket at the mortuary. Brother Ron, who was about 14 at the time, stood next to me as we looked at the man who had been so vibrant and lusting for life only a few days before. Ron's emphatic words ring in my ears to this very day. He gritted his teeth with utmost determination and forcefully said, "I'm going to be just like him." His life thereafter proved <u>that</u> avowal to be truly prophetic.

Ron had idolized Joe, and his determination to, in effect, be his clone, manifested itself in many ways. Ron, too, was a "dropout" at school. I believe he completed the eighth grade.

Each of the five boys in our family was required to start working at Dad's service station—we called it "the gas station"—at age twelve, when not in school. Since our father had had very little education, I don't think it troubled him very much when one of the boys left school. They could then work full-time for him without pay. He did not urge us to quit school, however. Two of us went on to earn our college degrees and one completed high school. Not so with Joe and Ron, however. Not that advanced education, per se, is the badge of achievement or the guarantee of a better life. Where would we be if no one were willing to perform manual labor? No, I certainly do *not* demean those of lesser education, provided they assume the normal responsibilities of life—another quality that education alone will not provide.

Back to Black Sheep II (a title Ron actually prizes).

In temperament, attitude and personality, Ron did, indeed, fulfill his vow to become "another Joe." He was, however, unlike Joe in some ways. Although Joe was a charter member of the S.R.C. (Sexual Revolution Club), he was never divorced. An uninterrupted married life, yes. Faithful, no. Ron's marital history was quite different from Joe's.

When Ron was sixteen, he fell in love with a nice, small-town girl of the same age. They wanted to get married right away, but needed someone to sponsor them. My wife, Anne, and I were the chosen ones. Lucky us! If we refused, they would simply get someone else. Anne and I felt that, given Ron's explosive temper and his immaturity, the marriage would quickly come crashing on the rocks. Being rather young, naïve and imbued with idealism ourselves, we hoped to add strength, guidance and direction to this fragile union. "Living together" was almost unheard of in those days; besides, deep down in his troubled soul Ron did long for the security and warmth of hearth and home.

It was not to be. The marriage lasted long enough for them to add several little Balensiefers to the clan (four, I think). Hobbles were for cattle, according to Ron, and the marriage became hobbles and tethers. Nor could he contain his innate hostility.

To spare the reader the unpleasant details or Ron's marital and extramarital adventures, suffice it to say that he had a grand total of seven wives. Happily, with mortality becoming a distinct consideration, he found a fine mate with whom he has remained married. His last wife, Bobbie, became *more* than his better half.

Many of us have, as boys and young men, dreamed of being a cowboy out west. Punching cattle; sleeping under the stars; chuck wagon meals; feeling free as the purple sage air. Ron didn't just dream it, he lived it. He got a job on a Wyoming ranch and was soon a bona fide cowpoke. He was a quick study and could do what he set his mind to. Despite his lack of experience, he was soon a-ridin'and a-ropin' with the best of 'em. I must say, I thought him to be a bit boastful when he declared that he could "rassle a steer with one hand while downing a bear with the other," but one could almost believe him, given his power of persuasion.

The story of Ron's life—or lives—could fill a book. In fact, he asked me to do his biography some time ago, but, from the bits and pieces I had gleaned, I suggested he do an *auto*biography. Besides, I would prefer to remain ignorant of many of his, um, experiences.

While in Ireland my wife and I happened to see a sweater with a picture of a herd of white sheep. There was, however, one black one in their midst. It was a natural for Ron. We bought it and sent it to him with a "no offense" note. He later called us, laughing heartily and saying that we couldn't have gotten a more appropriate gift. He wears the sweater *and* the Black Sheep title with considerable pride.

During this writing, we learned that Ron was given only a few months more to live. He has a long and incredible history of strokes and cardiac failure. On several occasions he came so close to dying that we made flight arrangements to Houston—but, as Ron says, Heaven doesn't want him and Hell's afraid he'll take over. He must be right. He has baffled medical science for years. According to top Texas cardiac specialists, he should have cashed in his chips long ago. His remarkable recoveries have been recorded in medical journals. He might well be called a Death-Defying Devil.

And, speaking of the devil, Ron has written a book that is so controversial (and frightening) that he expects it to "outsell the Bible." The Bible, incidentally, is his target. He rips its tenets to shreds and tramples mercilessly on every biblical scholar's toes. He asked me if I would read the *full* manuscript if he sent me a copy. He insisted that I read *all* or nothing at all. I agreed, of course, who wouldn't? *Big* mistake! I expected his thoughts and premises to be extreme, but what I read was *so* outrageous and antithetical to Christian beliefs that after reading about one tenth of the blasphemy I quit cold. I returned the full manuscript with an apology and an explanation of my reasons. Normally, I would *not* break a promise, but his comments were so sacrilegious that they must have been inspired by Satan himself. He asserts that the Bible is the source of most of the world's troubles—that wars have been fought over conflicting beliefs. He makes a *very* convincing, though heretical, argument. The devil is like that, isn't he?

I consider myself to be something of an authority on the written word, so from the thirty-odd pages that I read of Ron's <u>God's One-Sided Mirror</u> first draft I concluded that he must have had a ghostwriter do it for him. Ron had minimal formal education (I think he may have completed the eighth grade), but he was very street wise and shrewd, like Joe. And this is the incredible part of the story.

His spelling, punctuation, continuity and vocabulary are usually what one might expect from and uneducated person. Yet, the manuscript I read was *well* written, grammatically correct and the thoughts and convictions were presented in logical, reasoned form. Ron *couldn't* have personally composed the text. He must have been, however, the vehicle through which Lucifer transmitted his own philosophy. As Ron explained it, he would just sit down with pencil and paper and let thoughts flow freely from his mind through his arm to the paper—as though someone or something was "pushing his hand"—it was beyond his control.

Publication of Ron's book is on hold as I write this. His health is so bad that, about ten months ago, he was given two to six months to live. He simply defies all predictions of doom and, like the Energizer bunny, just keeps going and going and going.[*]

---

[*]After repeated strokes and heart attacks, Ron died a few months after this was written.

MEAN TO ME

Although I want these memoirs and musings to highlight more pleasant experiences, occasions and situations, I must include some not-so-happy conditions. My intent is to include recollections that might be of interest to the reader.

I have already given thumbnail descriptions of Joe and Ron. Another J.B. wannabe was cousin Arnold Balensiefer. On two occasions he nearly killed me. On one of those occasions, brother Joe helped.

Arnold was about Joe's size and age, probably around fifteen at the time of both incidents. I was around eleven or twelve. Arnold, like Joe, had an inner rage and reveled in confrontation. He would goad me and try to start a fight. But anger just wasn't in me, and I certainly didn't want to fight—just being Joe's sparring partner was enough for me. The sequence doesn't matter, but, as I recall, the first real scare I got was when Arnold held me hostage with a .22 rifle. I had just finished some chores and was headed back to the house when I heard the unmistakable ominous sound of a rifle being cocked. It came from overhead. Startled, I looked up and saw the cold blue steel barrel of the rifle pointed directly at my head. Arnold was sitting on his haunches on the roof of our garage, aiming the gun at me. He didn't have to say, "Freeze." The demonic look in his eyes and the cruel sneer on his face turned my blood to ice. He growled, "I'm gonna kill you, boy." I believed him; if you knew Arnold, so would you. I regained some composure—to my surprise—and asked, "Why, Arnold? What did I do to you?" Before he could reply, my Mom shouted my name and I heard the back door slam. The garage roof was so situated that she couldn't see Arnold, who quickly disappeared. She said, "You look like you just saw a ghost," and laughed. I managed a grin and said I was tired and hungry. I was afraid to worry my mother and more afraid of what Dad would do if he found out.

Apparently, Arnold had second thoughts about killing me. He downgraded his effort to merely torturing me. My most vivid recollection of this is the day he and Joe—for reasons unknown to me—threw me to the ground. While Joe knelt on my shoulders, Arnold took a garden hose and tried to force the nozzle into my mouth. I gritted my teeth, but he forced the water up my nostrils. I can still hear their diabolic laughter.

To Joe's credit, he did stop the torture when he saw that I was literally drowning. This moment of terror was especially traumatic to me because, at age nine, I did, indeed "drown" in a whirlpool at Rock Creek, Indiana—more on that later.

Maybe they enjoyed being brutal and merciless toward me because I had the image and reputation of "a good kid." Studious, responsible, polite, never in trouble. I had traits they at once hated and envied. I hated what they did to me, but I didn't really hate them (did I?). Eventually, as I matured, I gleaned a clearer vision of their twisted psyches and felt more pity than anger.

They're both gone now—have been for years—so they can't defend themselves. Wherever they are, I hope they will forgive my having made these revelations.

TOO YOUNG

Teachers can have quite an influence on our lives—that's a given—and it often goes beyond our academic endeavors. I would wager that hardly a reader of these words would have any difficulty in calling to mind a certain teacher, professor or instructor who made a lasting impression—however good or bad.

The grade school teacher I remember best is Sister Consortia. She taught a variety of subjects, including music (which continues to be one of my greatest loves), but I remember her most for the strict discipline she instilled in us. We knew exactly where we stood with Sister "C," and she made it eminently clear that there were two words she *never* wanted to hear from any of us: "I can't." The slightest form of vulgarity or impropriety was, of course, anathema.

In college, I was privileged to study under Dr. Fields, a truly brilliant and perceptive man. One of his most memorable and prescient statements was that the clearest path to good, sound mental hygiene followed the footsteps of Christ—and this was said in a secular school—but it was in the late forties. Can you imagine what would happen if that comment were to be made in a classroom today? He would probably be fired, or severely rebuked, at least. In the Pyscho/Science context, even an atheist psychologist, sociologist or ethicist would probably agree. Stripped of religiosity, how could one fault any of Christ's teachings—or deny the clearly evident benefits of the Ten Commandments? (Okay, so you'd prefer them be the "Ten Suggestions."). I also studied the Seven Schools of Psychology under Dr. William Blakely. We had our disagreements, but in the end, he urged me to get a Ph.D. and set up my own Clinical Psychology practice. The confidence and trust he placed in me has stayed with me to this day. Perhaps the best thing he (and other excellent instructors) did was to instill the *desire* to learn—to be constantly curious.

Although unable to pursue postgraduate work because of marriage, change of location and dire financial straits, what I learned from Dr. Blakely has served me well.

Being the perspicacious reader that you are, you will have observed a gap in my chronology, and you will have questioned the title of this segment. My reasoning is based upon the premise that the dessert should come last—and quite a tasty dish was Miss Rich!

Memories of my high school teachers are few but vivid. Miss Wood, Mr. Peck, and Miss Rich. Remember Ma Kettle of the older movies? Or Janet Reno of more recent times? If you would add horn-rimmed glasses and about thirty more pounds of flesh and muscle to Ma Kettle—keeping her same stern-faced expression, you would get a rough idea of Miss Wood's appearance and demeanor. Or better still, if you can imagine Janet Reno compressed about a foot and a half, the picture becomes even more like Miss Wood, whose name must have been destined by her Creator. But she made a great catalyst in my pursuit of knowledge in the fields of English and Literature.

Mr. Peck, my science teacher, was a teddy bear; a fuzz ball; and all-around nice guy. He had all the excitement of a Bunsen burner, but he knew how to teach physics. In appearance, he was Art Buchwald without the glasses. Round and chubby; heavy of lip. A half-smile that never quite got there. But, thanks to Mr. Peck, I can now converse (with some proficiency) with a dear friend who is a renowned physicist.

Which brings us, finally, to Miss Rich.

My first two years of high school were at Fowler High in Fowler, Indiana. In my sophomore year, I was assigned to a young new English teacher, Miss Candyce Rich. It should have been a chemistry class, because that's what we had almost immediately! In keeping with my pattern of comparing my teachers with celebrities, envision Miss Rich as Marilyn Monroe, less ten pounds.

Let me first affirm that I am one of the three people in the world who has not seen the movie "The Graduate." I have, however seen enough excerpts, read reviews, etc., to have concluded that there was something of a parallel between Mrs. Robinson and Miss Rich. I don't know what Dustin Hoffman did or didn't do, so I cannot compare my situation to his. I *do* know that despite the obvious age gap, the attraction Miss Rich and I had for each other was strong and mutual. She kept me after class on *several* occasions. I must say I had considerable difficulty in seeing the blackboard through the steam—and I didn't even wear glasses. Boy! Could that girl conjugate a verb!

We couldn't meet anywhere. "Having a date" was but a ridiculous fantasy—and fantasize we did. We had to be very careful about time spent together after class, and we talked about the hopelessness of our "love affair." We could see that it was getting out of control, and that it could end in her losing her first teaching job—which she loved. It was a no-win situation. In desperation, one evening, misty-eyed, she sighed "Oh, Frank, why couldn't you be older, or I younger (she was 22)? Isn't Dr. Einstein working on a time machine? Think of it! We could change our ages!" She was losing it—I could tell. The little world of denial in which we had been living was collapsing all around us.

We somehow made it through the year without getting caught. That first summer brought pain, but with it also came the solution to our dilemma. By the grace of God, Candyce got a new assignment—in Chicago, far away.

In a surprise stroke of mutual maturation, we agreed to make a "clean break" of it. I couldn't see her off as she boarded the train north, but I stood in the shadows and watched her family giving her farewell hugs. My heart ached and my young face was wet with tears.

It was quite some time before the mesmerizing combination of Candyce's perfume and chalk dust became but a warm memory. My hope is that she found happiness and fulfillment. I did.

WITH A SONG IN MY HEART

A lthough my thespian endeavors had been thwarted by grim reality, my eagerness to be "on stage" did not wane. If another Frank, the skinny kid from Brooklyn, could do so well as a singer, why couldn't I? So my eyes weren't blue and I had no "connections"—I could at least *try*.

In an odd and indirect way, my work at the filling station contributed to my interest in singing (Mom loved to sing, too, and, to this day, everyone in our family is a music lover). On the filling station property was a little plywood-type "café." It had a large and loud jukebox in it and I could hear the ballads of Sinatra and the swing of Benny Goodman—as well as the music of all the big bands of the late thirties. "Begin the Beguine," "That Old Black Magic," "All or Nothing at All." I could see myself in a tuxedo with a floppy bow tie, a la F.S., softly crooning to some chick in the front row. I would try to sing along with

Sinatra, milking every nuance, while working at the station. I remember one slow day, when my ear was turned to the melodic strains from the café. I was standing at the end of "the island"—the raised section that held the gasoline pumps. I was doing my best to follow Sinatra as he sang "Night and Day"—I must have really gotten carried away. As I stood there—feet spread apart—caressing (well, gripping) the broom handle "mike," and putting my heart into "You are the one . . ." I was unaware that a couple of cars had quietly glided up to the pumps behind me. As Frank and I finished the last long note " . . . and daaaaaaay," I turned to the sound of applause. One of the drivers said, "Good set of pipes, kid. You oughta go places." (Believe me, that car got "full service"). I may have blushed, but I remembered those words when I first stepped up to a microphone not long after.

My first break didn't come to me, I went after it.

In addition to my crush on Miss Rich ("Candy," to me alone), there were, of course, other girls in my life, the soft and warm things to which I alluded earlier. The only two whose names and faces I can readily recall were Mickey Moore and June Love. (No, really. That was her real name—and ever so appropriate). Mickey was quiet, tender, but almost inscrutable. I never knew quite where I stood with her, but she was a doll. Unfortunately for me, we were from opposite sides of the track. Her father was a doctor and mine serviced his Cadillac. That didn't seem to trouble Mickey, but I was uncomfortable and somewhat depressed.

In my day, it was considered indecent—even vulgar—to use the word "sexy," but how else could you describe June Love? She was a cute, five foot two, blue-eyed blonde with curves that I never saw in my geometry book. Oooooo-whee!

True confession number two (you may recall the first being my sneaking into a theater and keeping my quarter): I wasn't fooling anyone. I knew that I could never be June's only boyfriend—she had fellows swarming around her front porch like flies at a picnic—nevertheless, I gave my share of admiration and ogling whenever I had the opportunity.

But work, school and rigid rules kept me from squeezing June (I like that) into my schedule. I talked to her at school one day, and we devised a plan. She would spread the word that she was grounded the following Tuesday—this would keep the other boys away. I was to go to the town library, slip away and meet her on the front porch of her home, which was nearby.

Tuesday's classes were a blur. In Literature class I was rhyming June with moon—and *soon*. In math class I was calculating the minutes until I was to meet June. Luckily, I wasn't taking an anatomy course.

My attempt to hide my excitement and to appear nonchalant wasn't quite successful. At one point, my startled mother said, "Since when did you start putting sugar in your tomato soup, Frank?" I told her I was preoccupied with the work I had to do at the library—which wasn't entirely untrue in that I was "working" on my exit strategy.

The librarian of our small town knew everything about everyone—and the comings and goings of each library visitor. The town parents liked her because she would report any mischief a student would cause. Fortunately, there was a ground-floor window near a study table and behind one of the bookshelves. I had determined this through preliminary library "research." After telling "Miss Nosyness" that I needed some quiet time to study, I sauntered through the bookshelf aisle until I neared the unlocked window. Making certain that no one could see me, I quietly raised the window and crawled out. It was a short drop to the ground, and I had positioned my bicycle for a quick departure.

June Love's big colonial home was only three blocks from the library. I think I covered the distance in about thirty seconds. I was panting heavily when I skidded to a stop and dashed up the porch steps. And there was June, as planned. She patted the seat of the swing on which she sat, inviting me to sit next to her. I was figuratively and literally breathless. She breathed into my burning ear, "Why, Frank, you're panting so hard, and your heart's pounding." Her hand was on my heaving chest. Actually, I think it would have been the same scenario *without* the bike ride! Although I recovered quickly from the effects of my hasty trip from the library, I broke into an ungentlemanly sweat, and my heart continued its incessant pounding. I had had a warm, close relationship with Candy and

Mickey, but June's nearness caused a delirious emotional explosion, the like of which I had never before experienced. She was *way* out of my league. I felt like a greenhorn cowboy, fresh off the range, entering a brothel for the first time. I tried to think of how Clark Gable would react to such an inviting, nubile nymph. He'd probably sweep her up in his arms and say something like, "We're gonna spoon to *my* tune, June"—but I knew I was no Clark Gable. All I could say was, "Sure is a warm night." June huskily breathed, "I'm very warm, too" (not that she needed to tell me). With her hand still pressed against my heaving chest, she leaned closer to me and put her full, moist, red lips close to mine. Her breathing was much faster now—like mine. As our eager lips were about to light a fire, I heard a surreal voice say, "Time to come in, June," as a bright shaft of light from the front door slashed the moment of ecstasy to shreds. Given June's, uh, assets, her parents were understandably wary.

Shaken and disappointed, I stammered a fumbling farewell and sped back to the library, slithering through the window just as Miss Nosyness came down the aisle. She was frowning as she approached me, but, just as she was about to interrogate me, the telephone jarred the silence and she went to answer it. I grabbed my books and smiled at the old witch as I walked bravely out the entrance door.

I began to feel unwanted, inadequate and inferior. Mickey was beyond my reach. June was more than I could handle. If only I could do something to impress them—and other girls. I had no money. I was no lothario. What could I do?

The answer came on a spring night in the high school gymnasium. A swing band had been hired for a dance and Mickey agreed to go with me. After a few dances, I excused myself and impulsively strode to the band-stand. Choosing just the right moment, I tapped the bandleader on the shoulder, introduced myself and asked if I could "do a number" with the band. To my utter delight and surprise, he said, "We were about to do "Oh You Crazy Moon," do you know it?" I said, "Sure do—just give me the key." By this time, a crowd had started to gather around the bandstand, some yell-ing, "Hey, Frank, what are you doing up there?" The bandleader asked for quiet then introduced me. A hush fell over the crowd and I saw Mickey working her way to the front section. Her rather stunned look combined joy and fear as she mouthed the words, "Good luck!"

I would like to say that I received a standing ovation, but they were already standing, so I guess I'll never know. I went on to sing "Darn That Dream" and my singing "career" was off and running. The kind and gracious bandleader asked me to join him at some other upcoming performances.

I can't begin to tell you what a thrill it was to hear Mickey, June and other girls scream, "Oh, Frankie!" The glamour and elation was to be rather short-lived, however. The song in my heart was about to become Benny Goodman's "Goodbye."

GETTING TO KNOW YOU

T he United States was gearing up for war. Dad left the small town service station and joined the military effort with Alcoa Aluminum Company in the city of Lafayette, Indiana—our new address. This meant leaving good old Fowler High and the ones I held dear. It meant having to adjust to a much larger school and city. It meant getting part-time work to help out while I finished high school.

The band, too, was performing at distant venues; places to which I couldn't possibly go. That hurt. I never saw June (or anyone quite like her) again. When I last heard from Mickey, she was in Dewagiac, Michigan. I found myself singing songs that only the lonely sang. I was blessed, however, with a sense of humor and an ability to overcome the obstacles thrown in my path.

When not in class, I worked at various part-time jobs to supplement our income. While others were having lunch at the school cafeteria, I was mixing chocolate malts at Goodnight's Drugstore. A sip on the side helped me survive lunch period. After school and on weekends, I delivered prescriptions and sundries on my bicycle. "Sundries" included such things as over-the-counter drugs and various items including bourbon and gin.

One of my regular deliveries was what one might call a "milk run"—but I certainly wasn't carrying milk!

Every Friday evening I would pick up my parcels at the drugstore, hop on my bike and head south across the railroad tracks to a tiny, one-room shack that had an abbreviated version of a front porch. Occupying most of the porch area was three hundred pound Mamie Brown, overflowing and old rocker—in slow but continual motion. She was the stereotypical Southern "mammy." She wore a red bandana around her short-cropped black hair and an apron around her bounteous front. I always arrived promptly at 4:30. Invariably, Mamie would affect a mean frown and say, in mock anger, "You got my gin, son?!"—then break into the most beautiful, pure white smile imaginable as I produced the treasured bottle. It became such a ritual that I began mimicking her—word for word, frown for frown. She laughed with such animation that I expected the decrepit rocker to collapse at any moment. She tried her best to engage me in conversation. She would try to tell me about the old days in Mississippi, and I would love to hear her heavy drawl—but, as always, time was my enemy. Not only did I have other deliveries to make, but also had to return to the drugstore to put the collected money into Mr. Goodnight's penny-pinching, greedy hands before going home for supper. One evening, however, I just couldn't tear off as usual. I had to take a moment to make a small presentation.

Mamie had told me how she loved gospel music, but could no longer get to church to hear it. She said it did more for her soul than gin—but she loved both. One day, by the grace of God, I found an old, discarded portable phonograph in the trash barrel near the drug store. I took it home and, with a little repair job, put it back in working condition. Fortunately, the local music store sold used records for a quarter. After an exhaustive search, I found "Old Time Gospel Singing." When I gave her the old phonograph and record, she was momentarily speechless, then she softly said, "C'mere to me, son." As I stepped closer, she actually got up from her rocker (a feat I had never before witnessed), put a hand on each of my shoulders and looked me straight in the eye. With tears streaming down her chubby black cheeks, through trembling lips she managed to say, "Hon—ain't *nobody* evah done nuthin' like this fo' ol' Mamie! God bless ya, son." Then, turning her head and sniffling, she reverted to her old mock-anger, and said, "Now git on outta heah, 'for ah do sumpin' rash." But I didn't rush away. How could I let the next customer see my red and swollen eyes? As I stood in the shadows, drying the tears, I heard Mamie's deep and mellow voice: "A-ma-zing grace, how sweet the sound . . ."

<hr/>

Jefferson High (called "Jeff" by all) was an excellent school, but there are reasons for giving this chapter the title "Getting to Know You."

I suppose one could say that I was too sensitive for my own good—but that's the way it was—and is.

Images, feelings, impressions are gleaned from minimal cues. Attitudes are developed from association and myriad complex signals we receive—consciously or subconsciously. I was too inexperienced and uneducated to comprehend the deeper psychological explanation for my feelings and the attitudes of others. It should have been no surprise to me that it was difficult to make friends. I had little opportunity to participate in extracurricular activities. Nor could I join any of the clubs or attend games, let alone play an active role. I don't know how I managed to do it, but I did get acting parts in school plays.

Every school—every organization—has it's own pecking order. Jeff was no exception. It didn't take long to see who were the leaders and who were the followers—or to put it another way, the peck-ers and the peck-ees. Parental community status played a prominent role, of course, in establishing the pecking order. There was the unspoken code that dictated who was "in" and who was "out." If you lived on the north end of town, other factors being equal, you were probably "in." I, as fate would have it, lived on the south side of town—and paid the price.

I actually liked several of the outgoing, handsome and rich fellows, but they merely tolerated me. I must admit to considerable envy. *They* got the prettiest girls. *They* got chairmanships. *They* earned their school letters. On the plus side, I did quite well academically, and most of the desirable girls made it rather clear that they would be glad to go out with me. Great! How could I take a girl anywhere? No car. No funds. But the fact that I had no community status bothered only a few at the very upper social echelon. Then I met Annette Kiger and Ruth Long. I always seemed to need a duet. (Probably some deep emotional insecurity, requiring a "back-up.") Both were attractive and had sparkling personalities. One had blue eyes and the other brown—and neither lived on the north end! It bothered them not at all that I was on the short end when it came to money, status and time. In fact, we managed to have some pleasant moments together.

My fondest high school memory was that of a Christmas dance. Funny thing—I don't remember whether I took Annette or Ruth—but I *clearly* remember that I managed to rent a tux and buy the girl a gardenia corsage by squirreling away nickels and dimes for a long time.

It's been proven that one of the most dramatic and effective memory-triggers is the sense of smell. We associate something pleasant or unpleasant with certain aromas or odors. Early morning coffee; frying bacon; new-mown hay. Pleasure is associated with these for most people. For me, after nearly six decades, the smell of gardenia immediately wafts me back to that beautiful night at the Lafayette Country Club. It was a bright, clear, starlit night. The ground and the trees were covered with snow and ice crystals. The band played a broad variety of musical selections, but the one I remember best was "Moonlight Serenade"—which remains one of my all-time favorites. Interesting, isn't it? That even the subtlest of aromas—touching the olfactory nerves ever so lightly—can instantly paint the clearest picture (and generate the attendant emotions) of incidents long past. Well, maybe not entirely clear in my case at least. I know that the girl who wore that delightful gardenia corsage was either Ruth or Annette—two girls who were to mean a great deal to me during WWII.

PART II

THE WINDS OF WAR

THE WINDS OF WAR

As I mentioned earlier, a part-time job I held during high school days was making drugstore deliveries with my bicycle.

One day, upon delivering a prescription to a lady, I was asked to wait in her entry hall while she went to get her checkbook. I could hear music from a radio in a distant room. The sound level was low, but I was very aware when the music suddenly stopped and an ominous voice interrupted to make an announcement. I couldn't hear what was said, yet a chill ran down my spine. Seconds later, the woman returned. Her face was ashen and clearly showed fear, anxiety and despair. The change in her demeanor was so obvious that I asked her what had happened. With a tone of angst and disbelief she said, "The Japanese just bombed Pearl Harbor—we're at war!" I do not recall my reaction to such an earthshaking announcement, but I shall never forget the impact of that truly historic and dreadful moment. I do remember this: my eyes followed hers as she turned to look at a photograph that was prominently placed on her hall table. It was a picture of her with her husband and son. The son was dressed in graduation garb and, with diploma in hand, smiling with sheer joy. He appeared to be about eighteen. It was December 7, 1941.

The bombing of Pearl Harbor was cataclysmic in many ways. Not only were over 1,600 sailors killed when the USS Arizona was destroyed, but also, the future of many of the living was to be dramatically altered forever.

Young men, from the rocky shores of New England to the sandy beaches of California, were either being drafted or were enlisting in the several branches of the military service. Some women enlisted also. Many nurses and clerical personnel were needed for the "war effort." The Army had WACs and Navy had its WAVEs. Defense plants had Rosie the Riveter. Hardly anyone's life was left untouched or unaffected by the war. Next to the cardboard sign showing how much ice (in 25 lb. increments) was to be delivered, another placard was increasingly being shown. It was deceptively simple. It was a red star, which we all quickly recognized to be the symbol of a son killed in battle. Multiple stars were not uncommon, tragically. Many times—too many times—I would dread getting off my bicycle to make a delivery to a home with a star. How I wished I were less sensitive. Had I been more callous, it wouldn't have bothered me so much. To the mother or father who accepted the delivery, I could only say, "I'm sorry," but that alone was often enough to bring them to tears. I wanted *so* much to ease their pain. I wanted to say, "It won't be long 'til I'll avenge your son's death." Instead, on several occasions, I merely said, "I'll be enlisting as soon as I can"—and I meant it. I could hardly wait. My brother-in-law, Bill Rottler, and my dear friend, Joe Hayes and I talked with unabashed eagerness about our plans. I simply couldn't wait for high school graduation, so I attended summer school in order to complete high school mid-term. It was the summer of '42. Bill enlisted in the Navy, Joe chose the Army, and I enlisted as an air cadet, with intense hope of becoming a fighter pilot. Happily, seventeen-year-olds were being accepted under certain guidelines.

My parents and brothers and sisters took my decision quite well. Mom, of course, was her usual tearful self, but she knew how terribly important it was to me.

Annette and Ruth shed a few tears, too. (Truth is—neither knew that I was dating the other.) My problem with the two girls, incidentally, was that I was so equivocal. I tried to keep them both "on the string."

The song "Star Eyes" was in the "top 40" at the time (made popular by Bob Eberle) and Ruth had eyes as beautiful and blue as Helen O'Connell's. As one might expect, I called Ruth "Star Eyes." (As I recall, she had a heavenly body, too.)

Annette was "short and sweet"—literally. About five feet tall, short brown hair, and sparkling brown eyes and an infectious laugh that came easily. Her father had died when she was quite young, and she was raised by her mother, who, sadly, was an invalid. They lived in a tiny apartment, the only part of which I clearly remember was the cramped entry hall; Annette and I spent considerable time there saying "goodnight." She was to become my "girl back home," although I would continue to write to "Star Eyes" Ruth.

THE SUMMER OF '42

I knew that the summer of '42 was to be my last at home for a long time—perhaps forever—but I recall no sadness, only unbridled excitement at the thought of becoming an Air Corps pilot (the Air Corps being originally part of the Army, then later, a separate branch called the Air Force). I could hardly concentrate on my studies as I prepared for early graduation. No cap and gown for me, however. While my classmates were receiving their diplomas, I was marching to a different drummer—literally. In fact, on that day, I was marching in deep sand and heavy fog at Keesler Field in Biloxi, Mississippi.

I had been inducted in Fort Benjamin Harrison, Indiana then sent immediately to Keesler Field at Biloxi, Mississippi. Never had I dreamed that the glamorous life of a fighter pilot would require the ignominious chores of boot camp. Although we were to become members of an elite cadet program, we were treated as dogface privates to learn the "basics" (ergo, we called it "basic training").

My first night at Keesler won't be forgotten, even if I should ever get Alzheimer's disease.

If I thought my life at home had been tough, my first days of basic training gave a whole new meaning to "tough." What I remember most about Biloxi—about Keesler Field—is the permeating *wetness*! I almost *sloshed* in my wet bunk the very first night. *Nothing* was dry. I remember my fruitless effort as I kept rotating the pillow in hopes of finding a dry spot for my head. I was seventeen ("going on eighteen"); naïve; unworldly; away from home for the first time (if you discount my aborted Hollywood effort), and already beginning to think that the only wings I would ever wear would be in Heaven—should I be so lucky.

Daytime was not only wet, but also foggy. I remember our whole platoon doubling over in laughter as our drill sergeant's shout of, "Column left!" was followed by a "Thud!" as he marched into a solid wall. We fell silent abruptly when he barked, "The next guy who laughs get K.P.!" I nearly choked—but I didn't get K.P.—not until an incident later. The "incident" was my failure to make the sheet on my bunk tight enough to cause a dropped quarter to bounce (instead of bounce, the quarter dropped on my wet sheet made more of a "splish" than a "boing"). And what a K.P. it was! My "job" was to separate edible beets from rotten ones. Around midnight—having culled *hun-*

dreds of beets, and truly nauseous, I said to my co-K.P. dogface, *"Never*, but *never* do I want to *see* another beet!" Nor did I eat one for over 55 years. My wife finally convinced me to try a small slice. I did. Not *bad*, actually, but not a vegetable I would ever request. Memories of that K.P. duty sill linger.

NIGHT AND DAY

T he Navy had its V-12 students and we had our ASTD (Army Student Training Division). There was the to-be-expected inter-service rivalry. I still don't know what "V-12" stood for, but we both considered our branch to be *the* elite corps of cadets, preparing for our commissions as officers in the Air Corps or the Navy.

Part of the regimen included several months of college education. I had the good fortune to be sent to Syracuse University in Syracuse, New York. The change was like night and day—the "night" being Biloxi, and the "day" being Syracuse U. At the university, we lived on campus in student dormitories. Our studies were essentially the same as other students, but we were more restricted. After the boot camp at Keesler Field, being assigned to Syracuse U was like dying and going to Heaven. We studied hard, worked hard and continued rigorous military training, but we *did* get some weekends off. Naturally, we sought what joys we could find. Many of my fellow cadets went to movies; went bowling; hung around soda fountains looking for girls. I went to churches, libraries, music stores. I was with the fellows all week, so it felt good to be on my own—but I did get lonesome. We all did.

My love for music lead me to a downtown music store. In those days, you could try a (78rpm) record before buying it. On this particular day a summer rain was falling and I was feeling rather lonesome as I entered the store. A fortuitous incident, however, sent my spirits soaring.

After listening to Sinatra sing "All or Nothing at All" and "Night and Day," I decided to buy the record. The store was rather crowded; the rain had apparently driven many shoppers inside. As I inched my way to the cashier, someone bumped my elbow and the record slipped from my hand and shattered as it hit the hardwood floor (records were made of brittle wax back in the '40s). A hush fell over the store and I could feel the shocked stares of customers. You'd think I'd broken a Ming Dynasty vase! My first reaction was to pick up the pieces. As I nervously reached down, a soft, white hand touched mine and I heard a dulcet, sympathetic voice say, "It was my fault. I wasn't looking. I'm so *terribly* sorry!" I started to say, "These things happen," but I only got as far as, "These things . . . ," when my eyes met hers. I tried again, saying, "These things . . . ," but she laughed and said, "You're beginning to sound like a (and we both said in unison) broken record." That did it. We both laughed, the customers laughed and the tension, too, was broken.

I refused her offer to pay for the record, but eagerly accepted when she said, "Couldn't I at least buy you a Coke?" Before leaving, I got a duplicate record and, in mock fear, walked gingerly to pay for it.

The rain was now torrential, so we had to huddle close under her umbrella as we walked to the drugstore soda fountain. When we had to jump over a puddle, she grabbed my arm and a shiver ran up my spine. Nor did she let go until we reached the door of the drugstore. We found one tiny round table with two chairs available, and rushed to it with relief. We placed our order but from that point on, neither of us was aware of what we drank or what was happening around us. Our attraction to each other was instantaneous, strong, and obviously mutual.

The table between us was so small that our knees were dangerously close to each other's. When they inevitably touched, my instinctive reaction was to pull back and apologize. She merely looked at me with a soft smile and said, "Don't apologize. It felt good." Wellllll—let me tell you, if we hadn't been so soaked, there might have been spontaneous combustion! She was *so* warm and wonderful—so beautiful. Her flaming red hair curled out from under the green rain hat she'd forgotten to remove. Her limpid green eyes were a perfect complement to her radiant hair and porcelain complexion. I could imagine myself singing to her *a la* Bob Eberle: "Your green eyes with their soft light—Your eyes that whisper 'sweet nights,' etc." Even her name was lovely: Penny Heatherton.

The next time our knees touched, she smiled as she saw me loosen my tie and remove my coat. Then she mischievously whispered, "What's the matter, Frank?" and laughed quietly. It was becoming increasingly apparent that this small-town boy was getting in over his head (which was swimming). She had that rare combination of sweetness and worldliness. Then a scary thought occurred to me. What if she was one of those girls I had heard about—"Camp-followers," I think they were called. They would lead a soldier or sailor on, then give some sob story and take him for all he was worth just before he shipped out. What if she'd planned the whole thing?! Nah—not Penny. The more I learned about her, the less suspicious I was. Not only had she lived in Syracuse all of her life, but also, she was studying *music* at S.U.! I found, to my great pleasure, that her tastes in music were, like my own, eclectic.

This was all just too good to be true. The icing on the already delicious cake was her inviting me to a dance at the country club where her parents were members. It was to be held the next Saturday and Charlie Burnett's orchestra would be featured. I felt I'd won the lottery!

All too soon, she glanced at the clock on the wall, jumped up and said, "Omigosh! I was supposed to meet my mother half an hour ago!" With a why-must-it-end expression, she brushed her wet lips across my cheek and said, "See you Saturday night!" I just stood there, overwhelmed by the magical event, and watched as she quickly floated away, like a ballerina, gliding offstage. The fact that, in her preoccupation, she forgot to pay the bill didn't bother me one bit. I could think only of the upcoming dance.

In a daze, I paid the cashier and headed for the door, mentally imitating Bob Eberle:

". . . In dreams I want to hold you; to find you and enfold you; our lips meet and . . ." I was sharply brought back to reality when an excited voice cried out, "Sir! You forgot your wallet!"

POLKADOTS AND MOONBEAMS

O n the following Saturday night (which took at least a month to arrive), there was a full moon and the air was clear and balmy. I thought, "It doesn't get any better than this," as I drove Penny to the country club. She had cajoled her father into letting us have their car—a shiny black '41 Mercury—for the evening.

We were so comfortable with each other that neither one of us was embarrassed when I sang "Polkadots and Moonbeams" to her. After all, the words could hardly have been more appropriate. "A country dance was being held in a garden—I felt a bump and heard an 'Oh, I beg your pardon.' " At the word "bump" she thumped her shoulder against mine and chuckled—apparently recalling how she first "bumped" into me. She had a marvelous sense of humor—an absolute *sine quo non* with me, incidentally. This trait was further evidenced at the country club.

As we danced to one of the slower numbers, we spontaneously edged our way off the floor and out toward the golf course. She kicked off her shoes without missing a beat. The lyrical melody followed us as we approached the green, dancing cheek-to-cheek. Ever the corny one, I couldn't resist saying, "You know, Penny, you really suit me to a tee." She groaned and said, "Is that a fairway to approach a girl?" Then I groaned. We embraced. We kissed. I should have used a scorecard as a memento.

I wore off very little shoe leather as I marched briskly thereafter. I was walking on air. The iridescent bubble was about to burst, however. Final exams were coming and I was to be transferred to an Air Cadet training base in Santa Ana, California. The Army really knew how to hurt a guy. Just when things were looking so rosy, I had to be sent 3,000 miles away. I had always wanted to go to Hollywood, but never dreamed I would arrive via troop train.

Leaving Penny and Syracuse University was another emotional experience. If our chance encounter was something right out of a wartime movie so was our separation. Although it wasn't exactly Casablanca's Bogie and Bergman, it came close. As Penny walked with me to the train rain was falling, as it was when we met. No umbrella this time, however, but in a way it was more dramatic and romantic. She was even more beautiful with rain-mixed teardrops streaking her soft, white face. She had a pained expression as I quietly sang, "It rained when I found you. It rained when I lost you." (I'll never know whether the pain was caused by the poignancy of the words or by my singing.) Nor did she think it trite or corny at all when I pulled up my trenchcoat collar, tilted her quivering chin up, kissed her softly and said, "Here's looking at you, kid." (I can only give an embarrassed smile now, but at the time—well, you had to be there.)

I think that we both felt that the chances of our ever seeing each other again were very slim as we said our final farewells. Regimentation required that military personnel were to board promptly, stow the flight bags and take a seat; so, with a rushed final kiss, I reluctantly left Penny and did just that. She and her many sisters-in-sadness waved sorrowfully as the train slowly chugged away from the platform. The tableau was funereal.

As I looked at the young faces around, their forlorn expressions mirrored my own. Each had a story to tell. And there would be many more to unfold in the coming months and years. "Uncertainty" was the operative word.

TAKING THE A-TRAIN

It was late afternoon as we watched the western outskirts of Syracuse fade away. It soon became clear that this troop train was not the famous "Silver Streak" from Chicago. It was apparently resurrected from a slow death in the twenties or thirties. As dusk fell, I expected to see the old lamplighter hobble through each car, lighting the ancient lamps. Instead, to our pleasant surprise, electric lights came on. The Victorian gas lamps had been converted in time to shed their glow and to play their part in the war effort.

Any padding the seats had was but a memory. It had fallen prey to the many and varied derrieres of travelers—from flappers to snake oil salesmen. The remaining one-eighth inch thickness did, however, protect us from the cold oak seats.

The wheels of the lumbering train must have developed flat spots from sitting too long. They certainly weren't round. Most trains make a "clickety-clack" sound. Ours sounded more like a "cha dunk, cha dunk" as it jarred our teeth. We soon adapted to it, of course, and our thoughts—mine, at least—were filled with anticipation, anxiety and reflection. We knew that we were headed for a Basic Cadet Training base in Santa Ana, California, but what would it be like? How intense was the training? Surely they didn't force neophyte cadets to go through West Point-style hazing, did they? Would we get time off to go to the U.S.O. in Hollywood? I found myself fantasizing about nubile starlets. And my thoughts turned to Penny. I wondered if perhaps she might be bumping into another cadet soon. I hadn't asked her to wait for me—it would have been a cruel request.

My reverie was broken by a welcome chow call. We didn't know what to expect, but we were now seasoned enough to realize that it would be something less than Beverly Hills cuisine. My request to see the wine list brought chuckles from everyone but the sergeant-in-charge. After that, we took our metal trays and positioned them to receive whatever was thrown at us. It wasn't our idea of "dinner in the diner," but we had learned to keep our mouths shut until we were given the "chow down" approval. When we began eating the nondescript food, I whispered to the cadet on my left, "St. Francis must have eaten Army food." Totally nonplussed, he frowned and said, "What are you talking about?" I replied, "Remember his Serenity prayer? 'Lord, give me the grace to accept the things I cannot change,' etc." He smiled and whispered, "Gotta remember that." We were to become friends as the days rolled on.

It was a *long* ride, during which I was to complete the writing of my first story, "Raging Afterthought," of the mystery/romance genre. To my considerable distress, the only manuscript disappeared. (If stolen, I hope the perpetrator made money from it.)

We were about to see a cross-section of the land we had sworn to serve and protect. The cornfields of the midwest; the wheat fields of Kansas; the towering Rocky Mountains; the Arizona desert—the varied and beautiful scenery held most of us in awe. Many of us were from the east or the midwest, and had never left our home states (or home *towns* in some cases). We were the lucky ones, in my opinion. We were slated for the land of milk and honey. Sunny, temperate, exciting Southern California—the state with *everything*—beaches, mountains, desert, sun-tanned movie stars and *starlets*! Our fantasies were at a high pitch as we saw our first grove of orange trees and smelled the delicious fragrance. Citrus groves—orange, lemon, grapefruit and more—as far as we could see, in all directions. This was soon replaced with a view of barracks and aircraft hangars. Pretty dull stuff compared to Syracuse U., but it didn't diminish our eagerness to endure whatever it took to get us through flight training.

THE WIND BENEATH MY WINGS

A ir cadets were required to prove themselves capable of surmounting all obstacles—both figurative and literal. We performed all sorts of calisthenics and gymnastics. Acrophobia, of course, was an anathema. As a matter of fact, we had to climb a three hundred foot tower, attach a parachute to a harness and *jump*! It was an excellent simulation of parachute jumping. To my surprise, I enjoyed it so much that I hoped to have the opportunity to do the real thing someday (I was to come *very* close to it a few times, but never actually received the "bail out" order from the captain.).

Having "drowned" as a boy, swimming has always been a steep uphill battle for me—and cadets *had* to prove their water survival skills. But perhaps I should first explain the "drowning" incident and my resultant fear.

When I was about eight or nine years old, our family—including some relatives—went on a picnic outing at a place in Indiana called Rocky Ford. It was located at the fork of the Wabash and the Tippecanoe rivers, and was aptly named. It was a hot summer day and many were splashing around near the riverbank. Everyone was having a jolly old time with much laughter and loud chatter.

Never having learned to swim, I was quite wary. Water activities were spectator sports as far as I was concerned, so I just watched. While watching, however, I saw Dad wade out into the river. To my dismay, he dove in and disappeared. I expected him to pop up quickly since he wasn't much of a swimmer. It didn't happen. I looked around frantically. No sign of Dad, or of anyone else. The others had apparently drifted off up-river. I could hear their joyful yelling and laughter over the sound of the rushing river. I shouted for help, but knew that they could not hear me. Oblivious to my inability to swim, I waded out to the spot where Dad had disappeared. To my surprise, I found the river to be only about three feet deep, so my head was above the water. I drew a deep breath and, with eyes wide open, ducked my head under the water, walking down-river and feeling around as I did so. All of a sudden I felt an overpowering "tugging" at my body. In mind-shattering panic, I thrashed about wildly as I began to spin in a downward spiral. The watery grave to which I was ineluctably descending looked like shimmering, diluted orange juice, as the bright sunlight filtered through. With painfully bursting lungs, I lapsed into unconsciousness. By definition, I had literally "drowned."

On the riverbank a search party was quickly assembled. My father had come up behind one of the many bushes that lined the shore, after having drifted out of my sight. When he climbed out of the river and returned to where he had last seen me, his sister, my Aunt Sylvia, was standing there with a worried look on her face. She asked Dad if he knew where I was, saying that, several minutes earlier, she had gotten a strange sensation of impending danger. He explained that I had been standing at water's edge—where they now stood—when he went under water and floated out of sight. While Dad ran to my mother and the others asking about me, Aunt Sylvia felt an irresistible pull toward the whirlpool that had claimed me. As she approached it, a tall, bearded figure emerged from the swirling water *holding me in his arms*! He spoke softly to my mesmerized aunt, saying, "Take the boy. His time has not yet come." She eagerly swept me up and turned to carry me to my sobbing mother's arms. Dad and several others in the search party came quickly when they heard Mom scream. As they gathered round, she said, "It's a miracle! That wonderful man saved his life." They asked, "What man?" He had disappeared. Fortunately, both Mom and Aunt Sylvia had seen him, else they might have doubted one person's story.

After considerable speculation and murmuring, some-one finally said, "Pearl's right. It *had* to be a miracle. No one could be under water that long and be alive. Let's just thank God for it." Then everyone became jubilant and the revelry resumed.

In my heart, I feel that I know what happened and "who" it was, but, of course, we may never know.

———

I couldn't help but reflect upon the drowning incident as I marched in lock step with my fellow cadets to the ocean shore. Survival techniques included procedures to follow should we "ditch" in the ocean.

A huge ship was anchored just offshore. We were instructed to jump off it into the water, remove our pants, tie the end of each leg in a knot, catch air in the legs by thrusting the open pants overheard in an arc, and rest our chin in the crotch. (Later, I suggested we call this an "Errol Flynn," since our chest flotation device was called a "Mae West.") Over the years, I had learned to "dog-paddle" for short distances, but in no way could I be considered a swimmer. In a cold sweat I watched as the fellows in front of me boldly walked up and jumped into the ocean. How could I possibly do all that was required? Yet, failing this test could put me on the "washed out" roster. My stress level was over the top, but it was matched by my determination. I wasn't about to have my wings take flight before I had even earned them.

I was finally next in line. I briefly closed my eyes, said a silent prayer, took a deep breath, and jumped. It was like doing the parachute jump without a harness, and the jolt when I hit the water was like hitting the ground. Having spread my arms and legs, I didn't sink as far as I had feared. Instinctively, I paddled back up and, upon surfacing, looked around frantically for something—anything—to help me stay afloat until I could do the pant-leg flotation routine that seemed so simple when practiced on dry land. My strength was ebbing as I tried to reach the shore. I was sick at the mere thought of giving up, but I had already swallowed a considerable amount of seawater and it was either make it to shore or drown. *Drown*!? Not again! Just then what seemed like another miracle occurred. My right foot struck something solid. The ship's anchor was far from the ship, of course, and its huge chain was about ninety-eight percent under water. Each chain link was at least four inches in diameter, so it was easy to wrap my toes around one. With alacrity that must have surprised those near me, I managed to follow the required steps and was soon floating along with my v-shaped lifesaver. Had I cheated? Well . . . I certainly had no intention of cheating. Let's just say, "My guardian angel made me do it."

I could almost hear the ethereal words that followed my first drowning incident ten years earlier: "Take the boy. His time has not yet come."

LITTLE WHITE LIES

Our "training" was extremely intense, concentrated and difficult—both mentally and physically. Trigonometry was nearly my downfall, but I conquered it by staying on-base most weekends, while many of the cadets took a bus into L.A., which meant the stage-door canteen, Graumann's Chinese theatre and the renowned Hollywood U.S.O. Many romances blossomed on weekends, nurtured by the high drama and thrill of the milieu in which the lovers basked.

Not *every* weekend found me in self-confinement. I had a cousin who lived in Hawthorne, just south of Los Angeles, so Dan Hickey (the fellow I met on the train) and I bussed in to visit on a couple of occasions. Palm trees, brilliant flowers, tropical breezes—all so foreign and intriguing to us "easterners." We were treated like visiting dignitaries and were reluctant to return to the air base.

On one occasion, I took a bus to see cousins Ceil and Bill. It was a memorable trip, in that my dream of meeting a movie "starlet" finally became a reality! (Well, she *said* she was a budding actress and I had no reason to doubt her. She certainly had all of the physical attributes.) I thought, "Too bad I'm young and in the wrong clothes or I might convince her that I'm a talent scout." Nevertheless, I decided to at least test her sense of humor. After we had talked briefly, I put on a serious face and asked, "Can you keep a secret, Trixie?" Her already large blue eyes grew even larger as she looked furtively about and, in a stage whisper said, "I won't tell a soul." Then I, too, looked warily about, lowered my voice and said, "Actually, I'm a lot older than I look, and I'm a talent scout for the U.S.O. I had to take this bus because my Cadillac convertible is in the garage being customized. I'm always on the lookout for attractive young ladies to help entertain the servicemen." I expected her to say something like, "Sure—and I'm Lana Turner!" then we'd both laugh. But my little joke didn't get the intended results. Instead, with bigger than ever sparkling eyes and red lips wide apart she said, "Reeeeally? Wow!!" She *believed* me! What to do? I decided to find a way out without hurting her feelings, so I said, "Of course, the talent agency hires only the most professional performers. You look like an actress, so you don't sing and dance, do you?" To my surprise— again—she said, "Oh yeeessss! I've won dance contests and I *love* to sing." Hoping to trap her, I asked, "With all that talent and your beauty and all—why are you riding a bus out here in the sticks?" She paused, lowered her eyes and said, "Funny thing—*my* car's in the garage, too. I came out on the bus to visit my aunt. Besides, you can meet very interesting people on a bus!" Now I was trapped—but I was soon saved by the bus bell. Trixie, in a panic, said, "This is my stop. *Pleeeeeze* call me." She quickly scribbled her number on a card. Handing it to me, she ran her fingers up my sleeve. Whooooeeee!

When I returned to the air base, I must confess that I felt rather guilty about my little white lie. Trixie would probably be expecting a call *and* an audition.

In a fortuitous turn of events, I was absolved of my guilt and dilemma by—of all "people"—Uncle Sam. Only a few days had elapsed before I was informed that I had passed all of my tests and would soon be sent to Kingman, Arizona for gunnery school training, preliminary to being assigned to a B-24 bomber crew. I called Trixie and told her another little white lie. I said that my function as U.S.O. talent scout had been changed to Bombardier, and that I was being shipped out immediately. She said, "Oh, *no!*" and started to cry. I told her that I still had connections, and that I would spread the word about her talent and her other attributes. This mollified her enough to let me bow out rather gracefully. Truth is, I *did* follow through by calling the U.S.O. in Hollywood. I gave them her number and breathed a deep sigh of relief. Not only was I off the hook, but I also felt that I might have done the poor kid a real service. Didn't ever see her on the U.S.O. circuit, however. But, I'm sure *someone* made good use of her "talents."

JUST ONE OF THOSE THINGS

E very bomber crew trainee was required to become proficient in the various types of gunnery: handguns, rifles, shotguns and 50 caliber machine guns. Bombers were heavily equipped with the monstrous, noisy, teeth-jarring 50 caliber machine guns, of course, since they were to be our defense against enemy aircraft.

To develop firing skills, we boarded training planes and climbed to high altitudes to fire tracer bullets at a flying target. The target was a long, narrow cloth trailing behind another plane, far from our own, flying a parallel path. It was much like the advertising banners we sometimes see being towed behind a small airplane. The first time I saw my tracer shells arc high into the distance and hit the target, I thought, "That could have been a German Messerschmidt or a Jap Zero fighter!" It was high adrenaline time.

On the ground, we were driven to a firing range far into the desert near Kingman, Arizona. Several of us won our Sharpshooter medals the first week out, but our shoulders were nearly pulverized from the kick of the high-powered guns. And I thought I'd surely get tendonitis from firing the heavy .45 pistols. We even did skeet shooting—but from the bed of a *moving* pick-up truck. Now *that* was a challenge. The sound of the various big guns was so loud and percussive that it's a wonder we weren't deaf by the time we'd completed the course. And, being young and foolish, it never occurred to any of us to wear earplugs.

Some people have an arrogance and abrasiveness that is hard to abide. Vincent Mangione—a fellow cadet—had all of that and more. He was the stereotypical Sicilian, but taller and more muscular. He had shiny black hair, heavy black eyebrows and piercing dark eyes. He wore a perpetual sneer of contempt, unless, of course, he was in the presence of an officer. He could play his demeanor like a violin. Vince was a thorn in the side of most of us, but he had taken a particular disliking to me—for some reason that I couldn't quite fathom at the time. (I later concluded that jealousy was much of the problem. He was an excellent marksman, and I was giving him too much competition.) I didn't realize just how much he hated me until a near-fatal "accident" occurred.

Target practice on the firing range was relatively safe. We had been given every safety precaution imaginable. Anyone caught failing to rigidly observe *every* rule was "gigged" (i.e. he was given demerits based upon the severity of the infraction). He would also have to march in a circle around the compound, carrying a heavy rifle. Shooting a shotgun from a moving, bouncing pick-up truck bed, however, was quite another matter. The truck took five of us at a time—two facing out one side, two on the other and one at the tailgate.

Vince had tried to goad me into a fight on two occasions, but the punishment for fighting was severe and became part of one's permanent 201 file (personnel record). Earning my wings with an unblemished record was too important to take *any* chances; consequently, I somehow managed to avoid fighting with him. I kept my distance after that, but one day he and I were assigned to the same truck, much to my chagrin. I chose a spot opposite Vince, but was dismayed to see him change positions with my partner. Since we were constantly at odds, this was a puzzling move. I tried to ignore him but couldn't avoid noticing the look in his large, dark eyes, and the malevolent, twisted smirk on his face.

As we drove past the many skeet dispensers, small clay discs would fly out and we tried to hit them with shells from our 12 gauge shotguns. Tracking the discs required swinging the gun-barrel, and, in such tight quarters, shooting accidents were a constant threat.

Standing next to your adversary under these conditions was very discomforting—to say the least.

Accuracy required focused concentration, so I was startled to see the barrel of Vince's gun swing quickly toward my left ear just as I was about to fire at a skeet-disc. I instinctively ducked at the very moment his gun fired (thank God for peripheral vision). I had avoided the otherwise fatal impact, but some of his buckshot blew my cap off and my left ear was slightly nicked. Because of the other cadets' intense concentration and the sound of their own guns, they were unaware of what had happened. I'm sure I looked ashen as I heard Vince say, "Got a little blood on your ear, Frank. Too bad about your cap." I said, "You meant to *kill* me!" But he just smiled wryly and said, "Hey, accidents happen—it was just one of those things."

I had no proof of intentional foul play, and the filing of an official complaint could have kept me locked into military litigation for weeks. Also, we were to graduate from gunnery school in only ten days. Consequently, I decided to drop the matter. I could merely hope and pray that Vincent Mangione would be shipped out to a different Air Base. And my prayers were answered! I was sent to Kirtland Field in Albuquerque and Vince was sent to Texas. Once again, I had slipped though the noose of fate.

ALONG THE NAVAJO TRAIL

T he troop-train that was about to leave Kingman, Arizona was a mighty welcome sight. I could hardly believe my good fortune in knowing that Vince Mangione would be heading in the opposite direction. I had had no peace of mind ever since his attempt (perceived, at least) to "accidentally" blow my head off.

My two flight bags were crammed with all of my clothes, books, boots, et cetera, and must have weighed fifty pounds each. My exuberance at the awareness of our departure from Kingman provided so much adrenaline that I was oblivious to the burden. Had the bags been 150 pounds each, I probably wouldn't have noticed.

Scuttlebutt plays an active role in military life. Some of the rumors were off-the-wall, but most proved to be fairly accurate. Such was the case with Kirtland Field, near Albuquerque, New Mexico. We had heard that that particular air base was at least a nine on a scale of one to ten. Such unofficial, subjective and generalized ratings included the food; living quarters; attitude and philosophy of the base commander (Colonel Milquetoast or Captain Queeg?); proximity to the city or town; BX (base exchange—like a large general store) and "Girl-Pool;" among other factors—and not necessarily in that order. As one could conclude, not many military bases came anywhere *near* a nine or a ten.

Every mile of the tortuous, teeth-jarring train ride was a happy one for me. I was keenly aware that I was leaving the ear-splitting gunnery school hotbox of Arizona and heading for cool breezes from the Sandia Mountains around Albuquerque. My euphoria was tempered by a degree of anxiety, of course. Who could predict what might lie ahead? This was, after all, our final test. This was to be our advanced-training school. Those of us who succeeded would graduate, win our wings and be commissioned Air Force officers. Pretty heady stuff.

Although the distance from Kingman to Albuquerque was about 450 miles, the trip seemed to take a lifetime. The train lurched and clattered and progressed at a painfully slow pace. At one point, a fellow cadet groaned, "Man, at this rate, the war will be over before we hit New Mexico!" We all shared his impatience, but we did feel a bit guilty about wanting the world war to continue so that we could see action in Europe or wherever out assignments would lead.

We looked forward to each meal as a welcome activity. The trip to the mess hall (a converted old dining car) at least broke the monotony and gave us a change of pace. "Dining" was another story. The china, crystal and silver of civilian life were as "converted" as the old dining car. Our "silver" was some dull metal alloy: our "crystal" was whatever passed for plastic in those days and our "china" was a divided metal tray. As we proceeded through the chow line, food was unceremoniously tossed at our trays. A cafeteria it was not. In a cafeteria one has many choices. In the chow line we had two: take it—or leave it. Actually, the food wasn't always bad, but peer-pressure required us to complain a lot. It seemed to be part of an unwritten military code. Just when we had about decided that Kirtland Field had to be only the figment of someone's over-zealous imagination, we were given orders to prepare to disembark. There really *was* an Albuquerque. We could see the city lights twinkling under a starlit sky as the old troop-train labored across mountainous terrain. We knew that the sight of the city meant that the airfield had to be close at hand.

The scuttlebutt we'd picked up in Kingman was true. Kirkland Field more than met our expectations. We were assigned to real, two-story barracks. Having heard so many horror stories of soldiers in tents that were too hot, too cold or too wet, we felt especially privileged.

We quickly adapted to a regimen of calisthenics, crash courses, college-level classes, chow and communications—all between reveille and lights-out. We traveled our own "seven C's" and they were pretty choppy at times. In addition to trigonometry, ballistics, ordinance, and other courses related to bombing, we bombardier trainees had to study navigation, meteorology, rules of war and other topics associated with officers' training.

Despite our singing, "Off we go, into the wild blue yonder . . ." as we marched in cadence, it seemed that the day when we would be in a *real* airplane (instead of a simulator) would never come. I found myself making a parody of the Air Corps song. Part of it was: "Off we go, into the classroom yonder—learning math, oh what a bore . . ." But the day did come, of course, and we were finally assigned to twin-engine advanced trainers called AT Elevens.

FLY ME TO THE MOON

Our airplanes were relatively small compared to the bombers we would eventually use in combat. They were, however, ideally suited and equipped for our two-fold purpose—bombing and navigation practice. Several 200-pound practice bombs were at the ready in each bomb bay.

Two considerations troubled me. One was my feeling of inadequacy at navigation and the other was the fact that much of our bombing was to be done at *night*—the target being a small, illuminated circle in the desert. Also, we each had a camera that we had to pre-set to activate at the precise second of the bomb's impact and explosion. If we miscalculated by one and a half seconds, the camera would miss the yellowish blast and we would pay dearly for the error in calculation. For each missed picture, we had to "walk the quad" for an hour. After a few misses, I became an experienced, though unwilling, "foot" soldier. My accuracy improved as my feet grew sorer. When I reached the stage of proficiency, I was required to demonstrate my navigational skills.

We did not use a sextant and "shoot the stars," as is done at sea, but rather we had to use a map, a compass, a circular slide-rule and a variety of dials on the instrument panel (for altitude, air speed, ground speed, etc.). My first full-fledged navigation assignment was a disaster—or could have been. I was supposed to plot a course that would take us to a pre-set position over the desert, at which point I was to drop a bomb. The pilot said, "It's all yours, Frank." You see, the plane's flight path can be controlled by the bombardier/navigator when the flight controls are transferred to the bombsight. Our crew consisted of the pilot, the co-pilot, the flight engineer and myself.

Night flights were usually fairly smooth, but on this night-of-nights, there was considerable turbulence and the tension was almost palpable. Plotting a course and maintaining an unwavering heading were chores best left to seasoned veterans. I was neither seasoned nor a veteran—just a lowly trainee on his first serious navigation trial.

Like other southwestern states, New Mexico is comprised of vast deserts, towering mountains and lush valleys. Towns were—and still are—comparatively small and far apart, with notable exceptions of course. Flying over the desert at night was like flying over the ocean—no frame of reference—no checkpoints. Accuracy in navigation was especially important under such circumstance, and I longed to see the twinkling of city lights in order to get a fix on our position. According to my calculations, we should have passed high above a small town about ten minutes earlier, but there had been no sign of it. My intensifying unease increased as I became aware that a mountain range was looming ahead in the moonlight. I hadn't seen it on the map. Maybe I just overlooked it—besides, we were high enough that I saw no danger of impact. I tried to double-check my figures, but the vibration of the place made it nearly impossible. We approached the target area on "a wing and a prayer." With my eye pressed firmly on the bombsight and my fingers moving like those of cellist on the dials, beads of sweat became tiny rivulets down my face and blurred my vision.

Eight seconds to go. Seven—six—the bomb bay was open and I shouted into the intercom, "Six seconds to bombs away!" A tiny glint of light caught my eye and I assumed it was the target. Just as I was about to press the bomb-release device, more light shone in the bombsight lens—but *not* the familiar circular target lights. They were *city* lights! The pilot and I shouted in unison, "Abort! Abort!" as I quickly pulled back and activated the bomb bay closing switch.

I seem to recall just a hint of sarcasm in the pilot's voice on the intercom when he said, "Nice piece of navigating, Mister Balensiefer, but I didn't know that Raton, New Mexico City Hall was our target." Word of the incident spread like wind-blown fire on dry grass. "Did you hear about Bal (one of my nicknames)? He darn near blew Raton to kingdom come!" The sting of such comments decreased as the number of foul-ups of other cadets grew. Soon we were all needling each other in good humor. "Needling" is a great component of camaraderie. Properly done, a needle can inject a bonding element that imbues a spirit of brotherhood and friendship.

SPANISH EYES

Most of our time at Kirtland was spent in the classroom; on bombing runs; on the parade grounds; in P.T. (Physical Training); and in our barracks, but our "barracks" were different from previous quarters.

Since this period in our cadet careers was *advanced* training—the next step being the dual thrill of achieving our wings and our commissions—our living quarters were considerably upgraded. Unlike the dormitory style we were used to, A.T. quarters were what could be called "semi-private" rooms; two men to a room. My roommate was a bright Irish-Catholic fellow named Dan Hickey, complete with a well-honed Irish wit and *temper*!

So much was at stake for each of us (for *all* of us) that we became bundles of stress, wrapped in a sheet of anxiety. Familiarity began to breed contempt.

The "little things" became magnified ten-fold. A classic example—one of which I am now somewhat ashamed—was Dan's accent. He was every inch a boy from Queens, Brooklyn's neighbor. His accent grated on my nerves like fingernails across a blackboard.

One evening, after a tension-filled day, we got into an argument over the correct pronunciation of the word "bottle" (Brooklynese for "bottle" is "bah-ul"—the t's are dropped). I know it sounds outrageously petty (and I'm embarrassed as I write this), but we actually got into a tussle over it. I don't know who gave the first shove, but the bomb that had a short fuse finally exploded. We finally called it a draw, shook hands—reluctantly—and agreed that the traits we had in common outranked our differences.

One common denominator we shared was our religion. We attended mass together regularly, and even went to a church dance at the invitation of Dan's girlfriend (he was a better student than I and therefore could afford to use his weekend pass to date girls while I stayed glued to my desk). He had met her at a church function some time before, and, when she asked him to a church-sponsored Saturday night dance, he asked if she might have a friend for me to take. This was a pleasant enterprise and a clear signal that his ambivalence toward me had tilted sharply to the positive side. My books would have to wait.

Off to the big city we went—by bus, of course—and what a city it was... The Alvarado Hotel; the dream-generating Santa Fe railroad station; the Harvey Girls; the Kino Theater and much more. The name "Kino," incidentally, was given to many places in New Mexico in honor of the fabled missionary Father Francisco Kino. He was loved by Indians and Caucasians alike for his selfless charitable works.

As the bus thumped along, Dan spoke glowingly of his girlfriend, Lily Montoya—how warm, tender and loving she was, and what beautiful eyes she had. Great, I thought, but what about my "blind date?" Did she have two left feet and did she wear coke-bottle glasses? Actually, it really didn't matter too much. What really mattered was the fact that Dan had welcomed me into his world. I felt this to be a pivotal occasion. Not the date. Not the dance. There had evolved and unspoken mutual respect for each other—even if he could never learn to pronounce "bottle."

The girls met us at the bus station as planned, but what was to develop later was most definitely *un*planned.

It seemed ages since I had been on a date, so I was understandably rather anxious—in the true sense. How in the world could I make conversation with a total stranger? What if Dan and Lily abandoned us and we became tongue-tied. I could just hear myself saying, "Uh, my name's Frank, and, uh, I drop bombs." And her frost-coated reply, "My name's Mary—and yes, you do!" But it wasn't quite that bad.

First, the girls were beaming with broad smiles as they waited for us to get off the bus. It was only a short walk to meet them, but it seemed to take forever. When we met, Dan took the initiative and introduced me to Lily, and then she introduced Dan and me to Mary (her name really *was* Mary—I could only hope that the rest of my conjured-up scenario was but a fantasy). With the trained eye of an eager Aviation Cadet, and with computer-like speed, I calculated Mary to be a seven point five on a scale of one to ten. She wore a typical forties-style dress and shoes and standard make-up. She did not wear the coke-bottle glasses I had envisioned, nor did she have two left feet.

Conversation wasn't terribly difficult either. It was especially easy at first because of Dan's ability to get beyond the "fine weather we're having" and into more substantive topics. I quickly learned that a good conversationalist shows a sincere interest in the other person, and asks questions that can't be answered with a simple "yes" or "no." Our discussions went along so well that I was almost able to overlook Dan's consistent and annoying Brooklynese ("Queensese" doesn't sound quite right). "I saw" became "I sore," and "weather" became "weatha." At least he didn't say "youse" for "you." The girls thought it was cute. Mary had no accent or drawl and her appearance and demeanor were equally nondescript. Brown eyes, dishwater blonde hair, average build, neat and conservative clothes. The features that helped elevate her rating to a seven point five were her pleasant personality and her radiant smile.

I could clearly see that Dan's rhapsodizing about Lily was thoroughly justified. What a lovely girl! She was quite obviously Hispanic, perhaps some Navajo blood, too. Around five feet three, her figure was surprisingly and uncharacteristically lissome and exquisitely graceful. Her shiny black, wavy hair didn't quite reach the collar of her colorful Polynesian-style dress. Her high cheekbones and soft, bronzed skin accentuated her most enchanting and alluring feature of all—her onyx-black, scintillating eyes. They had an almost ethereal quality that gave a refreshing view of her very soul. But I suddenly became painfully aware of something I should not have seen or felt. The initial cordiality began to change into something deeper. I squirmed a bit as I realized that Lily was admiring more than my shiny buttons. Her Spanish eyes locked with mine. It happened so suddenly and so powerfully that it caught me off-balance and made me somewhat light-headed. Fortunately, Dan and Mary were talking together when it happened. Could it have been my over-active imagination? Were her soul-searching eyes trying to tell me something? Nah! Couldn't be. Dan had made it clear that she was pure as the driven snow. He felt lucky if she would even let him hold her hand in a movie theater. And we had just met such a short time ago. Two things worried me. One was the feeling that butterflies were practicing barrel-roles and loops in my stomach; the other was that she might do it again. Fortunately, that fear was unfounded. She had experienced an epiphany, but knew that it could go nowhere. Consequently, she paid closer attention to Dan, avoided eye contact with me—as much as possible—and carefully avoided being left alone with me. It was as though she was afraid of what might happen—or was I on an ego trip and just imagining it? When we double dated again, I, too, found myself trying to be more attentive to Mary and fearful of ever being alone with Lily.

As time passed Dan and I developed an even deeper respect for each other. So much so that my heart ached at the thought of my coming between him and Lily. Then, one evening as he caressed the picture of Lily that he kept on his desk, he looked at me with a bliss-ful smile and said, "Frank, when this is all ovah, I'm going to marry that gul!" Instead of saying something like, "Hey, Dan, that's great!" I said, "Are you sure she loves you?" Dan briskly replied, "Well, I certainly love her and I *think* she loves me. She's just not the kind to show it. She'll come around in time. Look at us, Frank; we used to hate each othah!" With a flip tone, I said, "What makes you think I've changed?" and threw a pillow at him. He laughed, locked his fingers behind his head, and I could almost see the peaceful scene his mind was painting: a charming cottage, a rose-covered picket fence and Lily, looking out the Dutch door, waiting for him. And I knew in my pained heart that it was not to be. At that moment, I almost hated Lily. Yet, what had she done but coquette me with her eyes? She had been quite attentive, warm and pleasant with Dan. I had made no overture to her in any way. I had no reason to feel guilty—but I did.

⁓

Fate must enjoy playing tricks on us mortals.

Dan, Lily, Mary and I had become good friends. It became a foregone conclusion that our weekend pass was our ticket to a fun-filled time together. Occasionally, however, I would sense (and, at one time, *saw* in a restaurant mirror) Lily's eyes trying to penetrate the shield with which I had protected myself. I passed it off as my over-active imagination. Then one day, Lily said to all of us, "How about going out to my parents' place for dinner next Saturday?" "Great! Wonderful idea!" we said with enthusiasm. "Where do they live?" Lily's long lashes lowered a bit as she said, "Wellll—it's a *very* tiny town on an Indian reservation about 35 miles from here. It's called Pena Blanca. I can give you directions. I'm going out early to help them, so could you all come around six?" We heartily agreed and Dan and I said we'd rent a car and pick up Mary.

Going home that night on the bus Dan was beaming as he said, "Wha'd I tell you, Frank? It's working! She wants me to meet her parents and get their approval!" I felt a sudden chill run down my spine as I forced a smile and said, "Yeah, Dan—I'll bet that's it." I prayed he was right. I really wanted to see it work. I *wanted* her to love him—didn't I?

Dan and I arranged to rent a car and planned to pick Mary up around 1700 hours (5:00pm, but we felt more official using military time). After noon mess, however, Dan doubled over with a painful abdominal cramp and had to go to the infirmary. Whatever caused the sickness—possibly food poisoning—he was confined to quarters for 24 hours. Green-in-the-gills, he later said—just above a whisper—"Guess it wasn't in the cards this time, Frank, but you go ahead and take Mary." "No, Dan, I'll call and cancel," I protested. "Get outta heah, Frank! Don't disappoint Mary and Lily." I hadn't thought of that, so I simply said, "Take care, you stubborn Mick," and closed the door quietly behind me.

When I rang the bell at Mary's place, her mother, Mrs. McGinty, came to the door. I had met her on a previous occasion, so she gave me a broad smile but followed it abruptly with a sad frown. She said, "Oh, Frank, you wouldn't believe what happened! You know our gravel driveway? Well, in a rush to get ready, Mary slipped on it and banged her arm up something awful! I took her to emergency and they put it in a sling. She took a strong painkiller and went to bed. She said to tell you she wanted to call Lily and tell her, but her folks have no phone." I expressed my sympathy and walked numbly to the car. What in the world was happening? I was trapped! Lily was expecting the three of us and I was the only one who could go. Was it providential? Was it coincidence? And then the scary thought. Were Lily's prayers that powerful? Did she really will it to be this way? Surely not. And I would do anything to avoid hurting Dan. My mind hummed with conflicting thoughts—with many "what ifs" and "if onlys" as I left Albuquerque.

My storied navigational skills were about to fail me again. Dan had given me verbal directions, but had the written map in his desk. I, of course, left without it.

In 1944, the desert "roads" of New Mexico were little more than dusty cow paths with no signposts. I had traveled several miles north through cactus covered, lonely wilderness when I realized that I was lost! I did know, however, that I was heading in the right direction. Then came a fork in the wagon-track road. As a moderate panic began to quicken my pulse, it occurred to me that Pena Blanca probably meant white rock—or stone—or mountain. I stood on the Ford's running board and did a visual sweep of the vast territory. In the hazy distance to my left I saw it! Huge white boulders catching the glimmers of sunset. My course had been set for me. I took off on the left fork and bounced along for several miles before actually catching sight of a windmill—then a water tower. Soon I saw a tiny community that had to be Pena Blanca. My aching shoulder sagged as I breathed a sigh of relief—mingled with some anxiety.

I had no difficulty in finding the Montoya house. Lily's car was there—the *only* car in the dusty hamlet. There were buckboards, wagons, horse and cattle. I felt that I was in a time warp. Come to think of it, I hadn't seen one vehicle during the entire bone-jarring trip.

The few houses that comprised the desert hamlet were neatly kept, though mostly gray with dust. Chickens and other fowl were everywhere. As I slowly approached the Montoya house, I could see a curtain move slightly in each residence as its occupants surveyed the passing stranger.

Had there been a town clock, it would have struck six just as I arrived next to Lily's car. And there she stood, between the car and the house. In her bright Mexican dress, she transformed the otherwise dull and prosaic atmosphere into a garden of warmth and charm.

Strangely—or perhaps not?—she didn't seem terribly surprised or upset about Dan and Mary. Of course, she expressed surprise and sympathy, but, free of encumbrance, and radiant with pure joy, she took my arm and said, "Come. Meet my parents." It pained me to think of Dan's wish to hear those very words. When we entered the house, we were warmly greeted by Lily's rather plump mother, her straight and slender father, her shy teenaged sister and her bubbly adolescent brother.

The pungent smell of chilies, refried beans and an amalgamation of spicy Mexican fare fit perfectly with the colorful ambiance. The house appeared to consist of one large room-a combined kitchen, dining and livingroom and two small bedrooms. A candle burned before an icon of the Blessed Mother and many religious pictures and artifacts covered the adobe walls. The dining table was an ancient refectory style with an eclectic mix of odd wooden chairs.

The Montoyas spoke *very* little English, but understood a fair amount. Lily, the only educated member of the family, served as interpreter. She also said grace in English, but, at the end, she added something in Spanish as a tear escaped. Her parents each gave a pained frown. The solemn moment left quickly and the food adventure began. And an *adventure* it was! Never before or since has such intensely hot and spicy food passed my lips! Was this to be my initiation into their culture? If so, I failed miserably. Try as I might, I could not conceal my distress. I gagged; my eyes watered; I reached frantically for a glass of water. I tried to apologize for my nearly violent reaction, but my larynx must have been scalded because, although I mouthed the words, I could not speak! Lily brought more water and apologized for not warning me. I wondered how long it took to develop an asbestos tongue. Fortunately, cheese and bread rounded out my meal and the paramedics didn't have to be called (they couldn't have found the place anyway).

After dinner, the senior Montoyas urged Lily to take me out for a walk while they did the dishes. Night had fallen and a sliver of moon shared the black night sky with millions of sparkling stars—our only light. With each step away from the house I became more talkative, keeping Dan's and Mary's conditions as the conversational framework. But Lily said nothing. As we approached an old corral where horses were nuzzling each other, Lily paused, turned her face toward me and, with the stars accentuating the glistening of her tears, finally spoke. With the same eye-lock from which I had, until now, shielded myself, she softly said, "You know, don't you, Frank? You saw it in my eyes the night we met, didn't you? No, don't talk—let me finish before I lose my nerve... Dan's a wonderful fellow and a lot of fun, but I could never get serious about him. Then when I met you, it was as though a cloud had lifted and I saw the other half of my soul. I had never felt complete and fulfilled until that night. There's no explaining it. I just *knew*. I've tried, oh how I've tried, to avoid this moment—but it had to come. I dread hurting Dan, but—I love you so deeply, Frank." Then, with raw anguish in her grieving eyes, she spoke just above a whisper, as if afraid to hear her voice utter the terrible words. "You don't really love me, do you, Frank?" She turned her face away as she spoke, afraid, but knowing in her heart what I would say. But I didn't. What could I say? It was sheer agony for me. Even if I had the gall to forget about Dan's feelings—and I didn't for a minute—Lily's almost supernatural sensitivity received the correct signals.

Hesitantly I said, "I'd die before I would *intentionally* hurt you but, yes I saw your beautiful soul through those lovely eyes and yes, I knew what you felt. It touched me, too, but at first I brushed it off because you were Dan's girl. Then, later, I realized that, although

I loved you for the incredibly beautiful and wonderful person that you are, I was not *in* love with you. How can I expect you to understand? I don't understand myself. I suppose you know that Dan hopes to marry you. How I wish you would... I'm so sorry, Lily. What happens now?" Through subdued sobs, she said, "Just hold me, Frank. Just hold me." I did, of course, for a long time. We were both clearly shaken by the overwhelming emotion of the tragic moment. Eventually we regained our composure. I tilted her chin up, kissed her gently and asked again, "What happens now?" She looked wistfully across the desert, paused, turned to me and said, "I'll go away. I know that they need a church secretary at St. Rita's in Carlsbad. I'll tell Dan as soon as I can... I can't continue to live a lie. He need never know of my love for you." Then, still looking away, she squeezed my hand and, in a trembling voice said, "Go, Frank, go quickly—please—now!" I turned and, somewhat bewildered, I backed away, walked slowly to the car and, with an ache in my heart drove back to the air base.

Sunday morning found Dan feeling much better and full of questions. He found Mary's accident to be as incredible as I did. Then, in mock anger, he said, "You suah you and Lily didn't put a hex on Mary and me?" Then he laughed and asked what his future in-laws were like. I told him their accents were even worse than his, then changed the subject.

Dan and Mary recovered quickly and were looking forward to getting together with Lily when the bombshell hit—as I knew it would. At mail call one day a letter came for Dan. He gabbed it with gusto, waved it in the air and shouted, "It's from Lily!" As he began to open it, I stopped him and said, "You don't want to share it with all of these guys, do you?" He shrugged and said, "Yeah, you're probably right," and we took off double-timing it to our room. As Dan read the letter, his face became ashen and he sat in a slump on the edge of his bunk. "Bad news, Dan?" "Yeah. Lily's taking a job in Carlsbad. But the worst of it is that she wants us to be "just friends" and that—that she's in love with someone else!" But Dan wasn't angry—just heartbroken. After a short pause, he looked at me with damp eyes and, through a half-smile said, "I should have known... It was all a pipe dream. But I'd hoped that someday..." His voice drifted off as he murmured, "Wondah who the lucky fella is..."

I knew that I, too, would hear from Lily when she felt the time was right. The letter came quite some time later. I was almost afraid to open it; afraid that her will to conquer her feelings might have weakened. What the letter said left me thunderstruck!

The letter was, indeed, from Carlsbad, and on St. Rita's Church stationary. She said that she had found happiness and fulfillment at last. She had decided to be a "bride of Christ." She had been accepted into a religious order of nuns. She closed the letter with, "In Christ's love," then signed it with her chillingly revealing new name, Sister Dolorosa (Sister of Sorrow).

I wept, but knew that we were both exactly where we should be—in God's plan. The years to follow would prove it so.

ON EAGLE WINGS

Half of my military career was spent at Kirtland Field, but the eighteen months of intense training passed rather quickly. We were kept busy during the week, and, when we got a weekend pass, time seemed to accelerate even more. With Lily out of the picture, Dan started dating Mary McGinty. They tried to get another blind date for me, but I declined the offer with several flimsy excuses. Instead of dating, and being something of a "loner," I visited museums, churches, other points of interest *and* the city library. Oh, yes, the library—quiet tables on which I could write to Annette and Ruth. It had current magazines and newspapers, by which I gleaned information about the war's progress in Europe. I read about our fruitful collaboration with England. All of the media showed pictures of our B-17, B-24, and British Lancasters bombarding Germany with tons of explosives.

It became "Walter Mitty"* time for me. There I was—an Air Force major, working hand-in-glove with chaps in the Royal Air Force. We had just finished an 0200 breakfast of bangers and toast, and were in the briefing room. Wing Commander Reginald Chewsbury's penetrating gray eyes swept the room as complete silence followed. "Men, I cannot overemphasize the importance of the mission you are about to undertake. The munitions factories in Stuttgart *must* be taken out despite the heavy anti-aircraft fire you will encounter. Flawless navigation and pinpoint accuracy will be required. That is why I have chosen Major Frank Balensiefer to lead the squadron. As you know, he is the most highly decorated Bombardier-Navigator in the entire Eighth Air Force. His prowess, his heroism is unparalleled, and we are *so* privileged to have him as our stalwart leader. Some of you may never return—a risk you have so valiantly accepted. But with Major Balensiefer's experience and skill, I'll bloody well wager *this* squadron will sustain minimal damage and will totally destroy the target. Upon your return, I'm quite confident that I shall be able to say, "Jolly good show, chaps—Well done!" Now, off with you, and Godspeed."

As we gathered our gear and strode to our respective planes, a young British Lieutenant approached me deferentially and said, "Major, Sir. I just want you to know that no matter what happens it will have been

*Danny Kaye portrayed this hilarious fantasizer in the movie of the same name.

my greatest privilege to have flown this mission with you." Before I could reply he dashed off toward the deafening sound of huge bomber engines.

It was through a blinding fog that we passed over the White Cliffs of Dover. I barked encoded instructions to my wing-ship as we crossed the English Channel and we soon saw searchlights penetrating the black sky over Germany. Suddenly, we were bombarded with anti-aircraft. With steadfast grit, I controlled the ship through my Norden bombsight. But, as I opened the bomb bay doors, the co-pilot frantically called to me on intercom, "Major! The pilot has been shot and my right arm is nearly severed. What are your orders?"

"We stay the course, Lieutenant. It's "bombs away" in three seconds, then I'll relieve you." But, as I released the bombs the plexiglass nose of the plane was shattered by shellfire and I was blown out into pitch-blackness. Barely conscious, I pulled the ripcord on my parachute, but it had jammed! As I plummeted toward earth, I heard a gentle voice saying, "Are you alright, Cadet?" Dazed, I looked up to see a lovely girl about my age with a bewildered and bemused half smile on her face. Trying to come out of my reverie, I stammered, "Oh—sure—fine." She smiled and said, "That must have been some daydream—or nightmare. I heard you mumble something like "stay the course" and "bombs away." You were so intent that it worried me. Hope I didn't startle you." "Not at all. In fact, you sort of saved my life." Quizzically, she said, "I'm afraid

I don't understand." I smiled sheepishly and in hushed tones said, "I'd like to explain, but I think we're already disturbing the readers around us. There's a soda fountain nearby. Could I buy you a soda or something?" She looked around, and then quietly spoke. "Actually, I'm the Assistant Librarian so I can't leave now—but I'm free in another hour." "Great!" I almost shouted; then, more softly, "I don't even know your name." At this, she extended her delicate hand and responded. "Jean Stokes, *Miss* Jean Stokes. And yours?" "Oh, I'm sorry—It's a tough one. It's Balensiefer—Frank. See you in an hour."

I went to the soda fountain early to get good seating. The ice cream parlor atmosphere was suitably furnished with small round tables and white wrought iron chairs. I made a fortuitous choice of tables. It was quite some distance from the entrance door, thereby providing me with an excellent view of Miss Stokes as she resolutely strode toward me. She was not a striking beauty, nor was she the stereotypical librarian. Her walk was fluid motion, but it was probably her only sensuous trait. Her soft smile complimented her rather regal demeanor. Having come directly from the library, she was plainly dressed and wore minimal makeup. There was a wholesome freshness about her that spoke of simple pleasures—picnics and hay rides; mid-winter sleigh rides. These observations flashed through my analytical mind as she reached the table. I quickly stood—noisily scraping the metal chair legs on the tiled floor, and then I swiftly moved to position her chair for her. Unfortunately, one chair leg was caught in the broken portion of a twelve-inch floor tile. As I jerked the chair back, the tile came loose and skidded across the floor. I nervously retrieved it as Jean remained standing, hand on her mouth, stifling laughter. I replaced the tile as well as possible amid repressed snickers all about, and repositioned the chair. Red-of-face, I again held her chair for her and tried to lighten the moment by saying, "Well, that's one way to break the, um, ice." Then we both laughed.

When, in deference to her regal bearing, I addressed her as "Miss Stokes," she said, "Please call me Jean." I, of course, asked her to use my first name, too—then the conversation was off and running with ease. I learned that she had just completed her first year at the University of New Mexico; that her ambition was to teach library science; that her father was a local physician and her mother a former educator. She had one older brother.

After digesting chocolate sodas—and each other's verbal resumes—Jean said, "You agreed to tell me about that most vivid dream you had." She seemed so easy to talk to that I admitted a part of my fantasy—the part where I dreamed that I was a Major and Squadron Leader. To her credit, she did not demean my temporary flight from reality. She did, however, playfully call me "Major Bal" frequently thereafter.

Jean and I became good friends—nothing really romantic—just intellectually compatible, with similar values and principles. Our relationship was short-lived, however. We had met only three weeks prior to graduation day. As the grueling days of training and preparation approached their end, I decided to ask Jean if she would pin my wings on me. I had never seen her smile so happily as she agreed, saying, "Wild horses couldn't keep me away."

It was a gracious tradition—even before the war—that a newly commissioned Air Force Officer could have his wings pinned on by his wife, mother, girlfriend or sister. Many of the fellows could only receive their wings in their hands, from the commanding officer. I felt sorry for them, and was thrilled to have Jean do the honors.

Jean's parents, whom I had come to know and like, were prominent citizens of Albuquerque and had considerable clout. To my surprise, they arranged for a photographer from the city's largest newspaper to attend the ceremony for the sole purpose of capturing the moment of joy on film. A fine job he did, as you can see from the picture below.

I've been blessed with many wonderful experiences in my life, but the day I received gold bars and silver wings ranks somewhere near the top of the list. My wedding day, of course, gets the Oscar, and college graduation is high on the list.

We shipped out shortly thereafter, and were sent to various air bases to become part of a bomber crew.

Before our actual transfer, however, we were granted a one-week leave. Misty-eyed, Jean saw me off and I could see her dainty handkerchief waving goodbye as the Santa Fe train pulled away from the charming old Albuquerque station.

I was fond of Jean, but I had hardly found my seat before warm thoughts of returning to Annette Kiger quickened my pulse. We had never stopped our correspondence—my relationship with Jean, Lily, Penny and the rest notwithstanding. It had been two years since I had been home, so the rough edges of the memories of my pre-war days were gone and only smooth, happy recollections (imagined or real) remained. I was in such a euphoric state that I had to fight off the Walter Mitty fantasy of receiving a ticker-tape hero's welcome. Any way you cut it, though, just the awareness that I was going home was about as good as it gets.

SENTIMENTAL JOURNEY

T he ride from Albuquerque to Lafayette, Indiana was a long one and it seemed to last forever. But, when we finally pulled into the station, the reward for the wait was great. It was a school day, so most of my brothers and sisters couldn't come, but my parents and Annette were standing on the platform with tear-drenched smiles. It was a joyous reunion, to say the least. Mom and Dad had apparently saved their food ration stamps to be sure a big homecoming meal could be served. In addition to my parents and myself, there were Theresa, Carol, Wayne, Larry, Ron and Joe. Marie had lost her heart to a sailor, had married him, and was with him on the East Coast. Millie had married and was living in Chicago. Vera had also married and lived in South Central Indiana and Leona had become a Franciscan nun, stationed in Northern Indiana. Annette thought it best that my first night at home should be strictly confined to immediate family. I agreed, but could hardly wait to be alone with her.

After the sumptuous meal, we gathered in the parlor and talked late into the night. We each tried to cram two years of news into one evening. Eventually, we drifted off to bed with a blend of exhaustion and exhilaration. It was good to be home again.

As if graduation and returning home weren't exciting enough, the timing of the leave greatly enhanced the occasion. It was mid-December and large, soft snowflakes had begun to drift silently toward their assigned resting places. The pinecones were especially attractive in their fresh, new white stocking caps. An almost palpable sparkle filled the air—everywhere.

As I gazed out at the fluffy white blanket on my first morning at home, I remembered clearly the way I had spent the previous Christmas. It was, of course, at Kirtland Field. I had not yet met Lily or Jean and was going my lonely way of study and work. Many of the fellows had girlfriends; they had places to go and things to do. So I decided to put a little Christmas spirit into my confined world. Dan was to be away, so I didn't need his approval for my plan.

There was a Christmas tree sales lot on the bus route not far from the air base, so I went there in search of the right size tree. It had to be rather small to fit into the bus and into my room. I had hardly entered the lot when a perfectly shaped fir tree caught my eye. It was about four feet tall and everything about it fairly shouted, "Take me home!" I bought it immediately.

The trip back to the base went smoothly, but as I wrestled the tree through the bus door and headed for the barracks, an officer—a *colonel* no less—approached. In the face of such a high rank, I instinctively saluted, dropping my tree directly in his path. With a frowning half-smile, he returned the salute, saying, "As you were, Mister," then skirted the tree and walked on.

Having purchased some popcorn and cranberries prior to getting the tree, I was set to decorate. I had some string, to which I attached a straight piece of paper clip. Alternately stringing popcorn and berries was a tedious but rewarding task. Christmas music was playing on my small radio as I wrapped the edible décor about the tree. After adding a few other decorations, I sat and envisioned a cozy fireplace while reading and re-reading letters from my family and Annette. It was a bittersweet scene.

As I stood at the window, my younger sister Theresa (Toots) walked into the room. "Glad you're home, brother." "That makes two of us." We then chatted about several things, including Christmas, before joining the rest for breakfast. My emotional, loving mother was so brimful of joy that she could hardly contain the excitement. She would say, "Thanks be to God!" and then hug me—repeatedly.

Although I enjoyed the breakfast gathering and the conversation, I couldn't wait to call Annette. She was completing her senior year in high school, however, so couldn't be reached until late afternoon. Meanwhile, my adventuresome sister, Toots (who had skipped school that day), came up with an exciting—and risky—idea. After breakfast, she took me aside and said, "Why don't we just go into the country and chop down a Christmas tree? Joe's selling used cars; I know he'll lend us one for a couple of hours." Ever fretful, I asked, "Gee—Is it legal?" Toots said that she didn't know or care. We'd just have to find a place where no one would see us and chop the tree at lightening speed. This was 1944, when the tree-huggers and environmentalists hardly existed, so I said, "Let's go for it!"

Joe, the original scofflaw, was glad to cooperate. He let us use a car with a huge trunk. We were soon off to the country, but the task proved to be more difficult than we had imagined. Every cluster of evergreen trees was fenced in or clearly on someone's property and off limits. But, as we wearied of the search, we spotted several trees of various sizes along a hillside near the highway. As I attempted to find a suitable place to park the car, I said, "This is it—our only chance. Grab the axe!" We dashed through the snow, up the hillside and quickly selected a seven-foot pine. Toots kept watch as I wielded the sharp axe. Just as the tree started to fall she shouted, "Omigosh! The cops!" We were somewhat hidden, so we were briefly out of their line of sight. I barked, "Hold the tree up! Stand behind it while I go to the car." I rushed to the car before being spotted. Soon the patrol car rolled up behind, lights flashing. "Got a problem?" the stone-faced trooper asked. "The darned thing overheats sometimes, but it'll be fine in a short while." He looked around, and then said, "Watch your driving. These roads are slick," and drove away.

As soon as the patrol car became a mere black dot in the distance, I shouted to Toots, "All clear—but let's get out of here before another one comes along." With a sigh of relief, she said, "Thank Heaven! I was about to freeze to death."

We quickly stuffed the beautiful tree in the trunk. But how we wished we had a station wagon! Despite the spaciousness of the trunk, the tree hung out at least three feet. In a cold sweat, and burdened with guilt, I took back roads and alleyways while speedily wending the way home.

We all agreed that it was one of the most perfect trees we had ever seen.

We had a player piano that used perforated paper rolls. As someone pumped the foot pedals and the keys danced to the tune of "I'll Be Home for Christmas," we finished the decorating by attaching a cloth angel with blonde hair (not unlike Theresa's). But, before doing so, I had pinned a small piece of paper on its front. It simply said, "Toots."

I had finally reached Annette and arranged to get together. Brother Joe had agreed to let me use a 1938 Ford sedan off the lot. As I drove to Annette's apartment, I began to get a case of the "what ifs." We had corresponded regularly, but we hadn't been together for two years. What if she had changed? What if there was another fellow in her life? What if, after having dated several other girls, I no longer found her appealing? With these questions still on my mind, I walked to her door.

Annette and her invalid mother lived in a tiny apartment in an old brownstone house. They were of very modest means—a condition to which I could easily relate—and Mrs. Kiger was a polio victim, using two canes to walk. She sought no pity and was the epitome of courage in the face of adversity. She also had the wisdom and graciousness to grant privacy to Annette and me.

With minor trepidation, I pressed the doorbell button. The door opened even before the "ding dong" had a chance to sound. All of my "what ifs" vanished immediately as Annette, on tiptoes, threw her arms around my neck. Her mother, balancing on her canes, stood a short distance behind, beaming with joy.

Considerable conversation followed—mostly in a question and answer format. Finally, trying to be as polite as possible, I said, "Is the Frozen Custard stand still operating at Columbia Park? It used to be the very best." "It still is," said Annette with enthusiasm. At that point, Mrs. Kiger smiled and said, "Will you two just get out of here? I know you can't wait to go." We each gave her a hug and left the apartment.

The butterflies were gone; the doubts erased. I felt elated as I held the car door for Annette. This was the moment I had waited for. I was finally to be alone with her. The feeling was apparently mutual. Her emotions were as transparent as mine.

The bright glow of happy memories blinds us to the mundane realities—but not this time. The ice cream stand at the city park's edge more than met out expectations. Wiping a chocolate smudge from my chin, I glowingly proclaimed, "It doesn't get any better this." To which Annette replied with mock sensuality, "Oh, I wouldn't say that." My ice cream melted. So did I.

With the rich aroma of hot chocolate fudge still on our breath, we drove a short distance to a secluded area of the park. As I doused the headlights I asked rather rhetorically, "Why do you suppose they call a place like this a park?" Without missing a beat, Annette perkily shot back, "Because that's what you're supposed to do, I guess." Nonchalant in tone, I replied, "I don't have a problem with that, do you?" The moon was so bright that I could see her coyly lower her eyes as she said, "Whatever you say, Lieutenant—whatever you say." It was a cold winter night, but the only reason I knew it to be was the sight of the thermometer on the town bank as we drove by earlier. Nor was Annette aware of any chill in the air, despite the fact that our breath was as visible as teakettle steam.

Ever so willing and eager, Annette put her head back and looked at me with thrill and expectancy in her soft dark eyes. "Remember, I'm an officer and a gentleman," I said huskily, leaving my post at the steering wheel and leaning heavily toward her beckoning, full lips. At that instant, she screamed as the car seat broke from its front mooring and sent us crashing backward. To make matters worse, my head hit hers and snapped her neck back with an audible "crack." "Annette! You're hurt! Is your neck alright?" She rotated her head slightly, wincing in pain. "Ooooh, it does hurt, but I think I'll be okay." "We'd better apply an ice pack right away. I'll take you home as fast as I can."

As we headed for her apartment, I speculated on the cause of the accident. Obviously, the front of the seat had not been secured to the floor. Under normal conditions, the problem would not be noticed, but with backwards pressure, it would break loose and suddenly fall back. Was this really an accident, or was it planned? A terrible thought, but with brother Joe's penchant for staging practical jokes, removing the nuts from the seat-holding bolts was not out of the realm of probability. I could almost hear his laugh as he formulated the hilarious (to him) scenario—or was I being unfair in my presumptions?

Mrs. Kiger was already asleep when we arrived at the apartment, so we quietly took ice from the refrigerator, made a pack and applied it to Annette's neck. She took two aspirin and soon drowsily announced that the pain was subsiding. She brushed off my profuse apologies, stating firmly that it was *not* my fault. Then, affecting a dour expression, through gritted teeth she said, " But I must say, you are a real pain in the neck, Frank." "Ouch!" I replied.

After assuring her of *safe* transportation thereafter, I kissed her lightly and walked quietly into the cold night.

Supposing the accident *was* planned? What if Annette's neck had been broken, as, for a moment, I had feared? "You're a lucky fellow, Frank," I thought. "Welcome home."

With the exception of some residual stiffness in her neck, Annette recovered quickly and was gung ho about going out again. Before entering the car on our next date, however, she shook the seat vigorously and pushed *hard* on the seat back. I explained that I had told Joe about the incident and asked him point blank about his involvement. He denied it, of course, and feigned surprise—but his eyes told me otherwise. I assured Annette that he had agreed to firmly secure the seat, so we used the car nearly every night thereafter.

My remaining days were spent visiting old haunts, renewing old acquaintances, exploring my high school (Jefferson), and just talking with my parents and family. Since correspondence with my other "love," Ruth Long, had faded out, and since I discovered that she was going with someone else, I decided it best not to call her. I would confine my attention to Annette.

I wished that I could get together with my Jeff High buddies, but knew that they would be away in the service. Joe Hayes was an Army medic; Bill Rottler was a Navy electrician; Garth Norris was a B-1 Ball-turret Gunner in the Army Air Corps. But, to my surprise and joy, I found that Joe Hayes was also at home on furlough! We promptly got together and went hunting with our bows and arrows. We had become proficient at archery in our pre-war days, but Joe drew the line when I jokingly suggested he hold a cigarette in his lips while I took aim. We had great times together. We even double-dated several times. Joe's girlfriend, Ruth Jansen, was not only beautiful, but also fun to be with. Once, when Joe and I were alone, I warned him, "Listen, old chum, if you let Ruth get away it will be the biggest mistake of your life!" He didn't. They later married and raised a lovely family.

My seven-day leave passed as quickly as a two-day honeymoon. I was soon sharing teary goodbyes with the family and Annette, who promised to write faithfully. She added, with an impish smile, "Keep

me posted on your location—I may want to sue you."
At that, the ear-piercing train whistle quashed any
attempt I might have made at a clever riposte.

My sentimental journey had ended, but the war was
to rage on for many months to come.

AUF WIEDERSEHEN

The clickety-clack of the train wheels was a sound both sad and exciting. Sad, in that I was again leaving home, and exciting because of what surely lay ahead. I knew only that I had been assigned to a base in Walla Walla, Washington. (One theory about the odd name is that the founders liked it so well they named it twice. It should have been "Wallow Wallow" because of all the rain and mud.)

When I finally got to Walla Walla, I was greeted with bucketfuls of rain. I remember little else about the place other than trudging through downpours. I do not recall a dry day. Fortunately, my stay at "Dubya Dubya," as we called it, was brief and uneventful. We were shipped out to Mountain Home, Idaho, and soon had the answer to the question, "How can you do practice bombing in the Idaho mountains?" Some joker who named the place must have realized that he'd get a lot of laughs. I think the nearest mountain was at least fifty miles away. Our base was centered in raw, hot, desolate desert—miles from nowhere, ideally suited for bombing practice. Our quarters were quickly assembled, windowless tarpaper shacks. "Mountain Home" indeed! As we did our desert flights and bomb-runs, we could hardly wait for our week-end "escapes." The only good thing that I recall about Mountain Home was the fact that both Boise and Sun Valley were accessible by bus.

Two other fellows and I decided to take a bus to Sun Valley one weekend. The world-famous ice skater, Sonja Henie, performed there. Top movie stars and other celebrities considered it *the* place to be seen. Glenn Miller was soon to make the movie "Sun Valley Serenade" there. So what did we see when we arrived? It was like a Hollywood movie set all right. The grand and impressive lodge, the famous ice-skating rink, the fabled ski slopes. The scene was awesome—but where were the stars and starlets we'd heard so much about?

At the main entrance we encountered a uniformed sailor, and asked directions to the latrine. He paused briefly, then said, "Oh, you mean the *head*," before pointing the way. To our grave disappointment, we discovered the truth of the saying, "The Navy gets the gravy." Sun Valley Lodge had been taken over by the Navy! Nevertheless, we gave ourselves a thorough tour and fantasized about being surrounded by nubile starlets. One of the fellows had had the foresight to bring a small camera, so we took pictures—one of which I still have in my picture album.

Other weekends found us in Boise, where I met Marilyn Stone. I can still see the street, the house she lived in, the beautiful landscape—but have no recall of how we met—only that I was overwhelmed by her smoldering, incredible beauty. The best possible description of Marilyn would be that she could have been a perfect stand-in for Hedy Lamar (I hope the reader can envision that gorgeous actress). Softly waved, jet-black shoulder length hair framed a sculptured porcelain face whose description defied superlatives. Her cerulean blue eyes were shaded by swooping, long eyelashes. Her figure was svelte and graceful, complementing her facial qualities. On a beauty scale of one to ten, I gave her an eleven.

In retrospect, during the war, as I was shuffled from airbase to airbase, there were seven ("The Magnificent Seven") girls, not counting Annette, of course, with whom I had a very pleasant relationship. But, of *all* the girls I met, Marilyn took the blue ribbon for beauty. She gave me an eight-by-ten photo of herself which I kept until I married years later. (I'd forgotten the photo in my footlocker and my wife discovered it. End of photo!)

The pleasure of Marilyn's company was abruptly cut short when our group was given a two-hour notice to leave for the airbase in Casper, Wyoming. Not only were we delighted to be leaving our tarpaper shacks, but also, the scuttlebutt was that several of us were to become part of permanent bomber crews—the goal for which we had been striving for two years. Phone calls were prohibited, so I wrote to Marilyn in transit as the train lumbered sluggishly on its northern route.

<hr/>

I never did see the tiny town of Casper. The U.S.A.F.B. was, necessarily, quite some distance from any populated area. Our quarters were only slightly better than those at Mountain Home, but accommodations and amenities were of little concern to us now, as the "big picture" came into focus. This was to be the time and place of bomber crew formation. We were all understandably anxious and apprehensive. I developed a case of the "what-ifs" again. What if I had another Dan Hickey situation? What if my fellow officers (pilot, co-pilot and navigator) were incompetent idiots? And how would they react under fire? What if our gunners were inaccurate? I tried to pull myself together and be more rational. I had found that there were very few fellows with whom I could not get along. Most were truly "officers and gentlemen." As for incompetence— our training had been so intense and thorough and the final test so critical that the incompetents were soon discovered and "washed out." This was true of the gunners as well.

My worries proved to be groundless. These were professionals—and *good* men, one and all. As each crew assembled around a ten-man table, the shedding of anxieties was almost palpable. There were, of course, nervous handshakes at the self-introductions, but the reassuring feeling of a common bond and of brotherhood was quickly and clearly evident. Each of us knew that we were now a team in the true sense—an alliance, a coalition. We shared one objective—to do whatever it took to help win the war. Little did we know just *how* costly that commitment was to be.

Had I been offered the privilege of personally selecting my Ship Commander (U.S.A.F. term for pilot), co-pilot and the other seven men, *these* fellows would have been my unqualified choice. As time went by and we learned more about each other, the strength of our allegiance grew. The lack of pettiness, the maturity and character of these young men was nothing less than inspirational.

There was a healthy spirit of competition between B-24 crews, and a sense of identity helped morale. We chose to call ourselves "The BOGS," an acronym for "Bombs Over Germany Specialists." We were quite confident that we would be joining the 463rd Bomb Group in England, and flying bombing runs over Germany. Our staging area was to be Omaha, Nebraska. Rumor had it that, after refueling on the East Coast, England would be our destination.

To prepare for combat, we had to make many practice runs under difficult conditions. Winter in Wyoming was not exactly a day at the beach, so it took considerable discipline and determination to be on the flight line at 0230 (that's right, 2:30am) in sub-sub freezing weather. We wore very thick and heavy sheepskin leather boots and gloves, pants, jackets and hats. We looked and felt like some toddlers must feel when an overprotective mommy dresses them to play in the snow. But many's the morning I thanked the sheep that gave their wool that I might live. The cumbersome gear was so bulky that it was difficult for me to crawl through the tunnel-like corridor to the Bombardier's compartment. What made it especially unpleasant was the nauseating odor of diesel fuel that permeated the bitter cold early morning air.

"Instant gratification" was a phrase we had never heard of—nor experienced. Delay, frustration and military are almost synonymous words. We had hoped to be on our way to Omaha, then England, after an abbreviated orientation period, but days dragged into weeks, and our morale was being adversely affected. The base commander noticed this and tried to break the boredom cycle. One morning at our "early-bird special" breakfast, I felt a tap on my shoulder. As I turned, I was startled to see a very tall man in civilian clothes. He smiled and said, "Morning, Lieutenant. What's good on the menu?" It was unmistakably John Wayne. My stomach did a barrel roll, but I tried to appear cool, saying something like, "I've had worse oatmeal—but I don't know where." As he chuckled, other young officers started to bunch up, hoping to write home about having breakfast with "the Duke,"

John Wayne. He made the encounter enjoyable and put us all at ease. He knew that we would soon be dodging flak over enemy territory.

The C.O. certainly must have had some clout, because it wasn't long before Rita Hayworth appeared and willingly talked to the fellows and signed her autograph for many goggle-eyed flyers. The Air Field became fantasyland for a little while.

Orders from Omaha finally arrived. The crisp air fairly crackled with excitement and enthusiasm. I felt like a racehorse at the starting gate as I jockeyed for position to see the alphabetical listing on the posted roster. I had to stifle a "Yahoo!" as I read down the list. BALENSIEFER, F.H. It stood out like a neon light, to me. My dream of joining the 8th A.F. Command in England was about to be realized. We were scheduled to get three days of intensive overseas orientation before leaving Omaha. We left Casper the next day.

Omaha was a beehive of activity. It was apparent from the somber looks on some of the flyers' faces that the reality of their mortality was setting in. Would they ever set foot on American soil again? How accurate was German anti-aircraft artillery? That didn't worry me as much as the fear that something might happen to burst my shimmering bubble.

I slept fitfully the first night. My throat was sore and swallowing was painful. By morning, I found it difficult to breath, let alone swallow. My neck felt twice its normal size. Frightened and worried, I rushed to the infirmary. It didn't take an M.D. to see that I was in critical condition. A stoic (and apparently sadistic) surgeon had me sit on the edge of an operating table. An aide held me in a firm grip as he lanced my inner throat *without* an anesthetic! The pain was almost unbearable. I couldn't believe what was happening! The surgeon's eyeglasses became weaving fog-covered lamps as I felt myself sinking—drifting—being stretched out on a gurney. When I awoke in a hospital bed, the first thing I felt was sticky red blood all over my neck and pillow. Not only was pre-op ignored by Dr. Dracula, but so was post-op. A nurse finally came by and explained that I had peritonsillar cellulitis. I had been unconscious for some time—*not* because of anesthesia (unfortunately) but because of loss of blood and weakness from the intense pain. But the burning question was, "How soon can I be released?" The nurse agreed to ask the doctor A.S.A.P. and went about her duties. Was my worst fear about to be realized? I had come this far. I was on the cusp of the dream. Surely I—the clueless nurse suddenly appeared, brusquely announcing, "Three days in bed, then grounded for a week." I wanted to scream, "NO! This can't be!" Instead I grabbed the nurse's hand and said, "If I don't report for duty tomorrow, I'll be dropped from my crew. They'll leave without me!" It must have been the pathetic look on my face that changed her chilly demeanor to a warm smile of understanding. With surprising sincerity she squeezed my hand and said,

"I *really* am sorry, Lieutenant, but since you can't eat or drink yet, the IV has to stay in." Then with some levity, "And besides, this contraption won't fit in your airplane." She added, "Incidentally, the fellows in your crew called and said they'd be in to see you the minute their schedule permits." With that she was off to see her next patient.

The deep disappointment left me feeling depressed, frustrated and angry. I couldn't help but say, "WHY? WHY?! What's it all about?! Howie, Mack, Les and the rest, we're like *brothers*! How unfair can life get?!" My mother had always said, "God has His reasons," but at this, my darkest hour, those words seemed so hollow and hard to accept.

As I lay wallowing in self-pity, thoughts raging and eyes closed, I heard a deep male voice gently calling, "Hey, Frank." I opened my eyes to see that I was surrounded by all nine of my crew—my buddies. It was a tableau that I shall never forget. As they stood there with their shy grins, I scanned the group and tried to speak. I shook my head slowly and said, "You guys! You..." Then I choked up and, to my great embarrassment, huge tears welled up in my eyes. As I blinked them away and regained clear vision, I could see that I was not alone with my emotions. I heard sniffles. Some turned their heads with false coughs, some were suddenly interested in the vinyl floor pattern. Mack made a fist and playfully hit me on the shoulder. Les said, "You must have made some points with the head nurse, Frank. She told us that regulations prohibited more than two visitors at a time, but that she'd look the other way if we were quick about it." We made an effort at light conversation, but it didn't work. We knew we'd flown our last bomb run together. The chatter stopped abruptly. Howie spoke for the group. "Maybe you'll be assigned to the next squadron, Frank, but let us know. We'll write, too." One by one, the men bade me a fleeting farewell—some shaking my hand, some hitting me lightly on the shoulder. Howie, the last to leave, stopped, turned, took a deep breath and huskily said, "We'll miss you old buddy," then hurriedly turned his face and left. I felt sad, empty and alone... It was the final curtain of a Greek tragedy. We were never to meet again.

On day three—departure day for my crew—I was awakened by the distant but distinctive roar of the huge and powerful B-24 engines. From my bed in the infirmary, I could see out a window to an overcast, gray sky. The gloominess of the morning and the awareness of my condition were worsened by the sight of the departing planes as they struggled for altitude. From a distance, logos and emblems that had been painted on the planes could not be seen. (Ours was "The BOGS," with a painting of falling bombs under it.) As I watched with heavy heart, I wished that I knew which one I would have been on. Then, to my astonishment and joy, one of the planes dipped it wings—a subtle signal to set it apart from the rest. Could my intense wishful thinking have caused me to imagine it? No, there it went again! It *had* to be

Howie at the controls. With a lump in my throat, I whispered, "Auf wiedersehen, guys." I closed my eyes and turned my head away. It was all over...then I felt a gentle touch on my arm. I opened my eyes to see an angelic smile on the transformed nurse, Carol. She gently took my hand and warmly said, "I know it's rough, but you'll do just fine. I really believe that there is a purpose for everything that happens to us." Her words proved to be truly prophetic.

Howie's prediction that I would be reassigned to another England-bound squadron had given me false hope. It wasn't in the cards. The startling reason wasn't revealed to me until two months later.

DEEP IN THE HEART OF TEXAS

After a full recovery, I was assigned to an air base near Fort Worth, Texas as an instructor. I was to train air cadets in bombing techniques, navigation and meteorology. The wind in my sails having died, I felt "all at sea" and didn't particularly care where the tide took me.

I arrived at Fort Worth with little enthusiasm despite the fact that the assignment was a feather in my cap. Although my feelings of depression and disappointment were understandable, I couldn't let them affect my teaching ability. In trying to put on a happy face, I actually did feel better. With some introspection, I soon doffed my self-pity and became more involved with the curricula. It wasn't long before I was listening to the personal problems of some of the cadets. In so doing, I was drawn away from my egocentric world and became involved in the fate of others. It doesn't take a theologian or a psychologist to explain that self-absorption is the bane of the soul.

The little contact I had with gen-u-wine Texans convinced me that they are warm and wonderful—this is a generalization, I realize, but I can still hear the "howdys" and see the broad, sun-kissed smiles. And their chicken with biscuits and honey! Why, Darlin', it wuz nuthin' short o' scrumptious! Unfortunately, what I remember most vividly about my time at Fort Worth was the intense, agonizing, brain-deadening *heat*. Having been raised in the Midwest, I was used to heat and humidity, but <u>this</u> was something else. I had often heard it said that, whatever any other state had, it was <u>more</u> and bigger in Texas. If talking about weather, I can vouch for that! One would normally expect nighttime relief from the oppressive heat, but not so in Fort Worth, the Hades annex. What little relief we did get came from taking our cots outside and lying next to a tiny pond. The warm water, of course, did nothing to reduce the humidity. Air conditioning? Never heard of it.

It was accepted as fact that some of the most beautiful women lived in or near Dallas—Fort Worth's neighbor and rich cousin. Ever a student of human nature—and of beauty in its various forms, I decided to set out upon a personal investigation. How could one city—or area—lay claim to an inordinate share of feminine pulchritude? Yet, the assertions were made far and wide.

By a happy coincidence, there was a bus stop near the Nieman-Marcus department store, where chauffeured Rolls Royces were as common as Chevys and Fords at Sears or Penney's. Ermine and mink were de rigueur in those days—nor were they rationed. I did a self-guided tour of the fabulous store. What a revelation. Crystal; china; furniture; *jewelry* beyond imagination. It occurred to me that the value of one floor could have bought many B-24s and a ton of bombs. But I was digressing from my objective. I needed to get a broad cross-section of the general populace in order to be fair in my analysis. Nieman-Marcus was hardly the place for a view of the common folk. I found an old-fashioned ice cream parlor with an excellent street-view nearby and, milkshake at the ready, began my rather unscientific experiment. I mentally set up a scale of one to five (five being best) to evaluate the girls and women I would see pass by during a half-hour period (this was what the fellows would call "rough duty"). The streets were filled with pedestrian activity. Gasoline was rationed, after all. And, since most men were in the service, women were more in evidence than ever.

To my infinite delight, the majority were at least a four. From teenagers to young grandmothers, I saw vibrant, stunning beauty. The law of averages brought in several ones and twos, of course, buy they were clearly in the minority.

That half hour seemed like five minutes, but the test results were conclusive. There are (<u>were</u>, at least) an extraordinary number of elegant, gorgeous women in Dallas. I didn't dare think that there was a correlation between wealth and beauty.

I kept telling myself that there had to be a perfectly logical reason for having received no mail from Howie, Mack or any of my crew—but it did trouble me. Two months had gone by—then one day, as I was crossing the quad on the way to the training room, I heard a familiar voice, "Hey, Frank!" I turned and saw Phil Archer, a bombardier from my class at Kirtland Field. He had shipped out of Omaha for England the same day my crew had. The grip of his handshake was exceptionally firm and his smile was forced and strained. He told me that he knew I'd been assigned to Fort Worth; that he was on a temporary disability leave after having taken some flak from anti-aircraft fire during mission over Germany; that he was heading for his home in Dallas and that he wanted to be sure to see me personally. It seemed strange to me that he would go out of his way to see me. We were classmates, but hardly knew each other on a personal basis. I said, "Phil, what is it? You didn't make a special trip to the base just to "Hi." Something's wrong, isn't there?" With lowered eyes, he said, "I was assigned to the same squadron as your crew in England. Before flying missions, we had a period of orientation during which I got to know Howie and the rest pretty well. You couldn't ask for a better bunch o' guys—"The BOGS," they called themselves. Well, the day *finally* came when we flew our first mission over Germany. I was in the wing ship, on the port side of your crew's ship. As we approached Stuttgart, flak was everywhere. I dropped my bombs and glanced to my right." He paused, and then with a grim look of anguish, he looked at me squarely and said, "Frank, it tears me apart to have to tell you this, but—well—I saw the plane blown to a million pieces. No one could have bailed out. We took some hits, too, but returned to base and made another twenty-two missions. But I'll never forget that horrible sight. A million pieces..." his voice trailed off. I heard myself mumble, "Thanks, Phil—it was really good of you to tell me personally. I know it took a lot of courage." With a heartfelt handshake he said, "Look—I'll be in Dallas for a while. How about meeting for lunch one day?" Smiling, I said, "I'd like that, Phil. I know of a great ice cream parlor."

I was late for class. It was *not* a good day.

That evening, sitting alone in my room, I pondered Mom's and Carol's words, "There's a purpose for everything..." Now I knew the "why." God wasn't finished with me yet.

❧

The buzz around the base was the recent development of the gigantic B-29. We learned that it was similar to the B-17, "the Flying Fortress," but *much* larger. Only one was assigned to our Texas base for our re-orientation. The technical aspects of bombing, navigation, engineering, gunnery—all were more complex and advanced. It required considerable training to prepare for pinpoint bombing. It was a long-range bomber that had an almost eerie aura about it. None of us had ever seen anything so large. The nose—the bombardier's compartment—looked like a geodesic Plexiglas hemisphere.

My dream of being assigned to a B-29 Super-Fortress crew (for overseas duty) was just that. My C.O. had implied that that was to be my next step. It never happened. As I was completing my orientation, we received the startling and prophetic news that one of B-29s—the Enola Gaye—had dropped a devastating atomic bomb on Hiroshima, Japan. Germany was already defeated. Dr. Teller's atom bomb; President Truman's dramatic decision; the bomber crew's heroic actions—these had turned the tide. On August 30, 1945, we had Japan's unconditional surrender. World War II was over! The ensuing "cold war" with communist countries was to drag on for decades. Our devious and counterfeit "ally," Russia, was to become our archenemy.

PART III

THE GOOD LIFE

BACK HOME AGAIN, IN INDIANA

In November of 1945, I was "mustered out" in Dayton, Ohio—why not in Indiana, I neither knew nor cared. I could only think of getting home and reworking my pre-war plans for a bright future.

The train to home played a different tune this time. It was, "Clickety-clack, you're going back." Back to Annette; to my family; to my black cocker spaniel, Whimsy; and to an exciting, unknown future. (The latter was worrisome, but there would be time to choose which path to take.)

After a joyful reunion with the family and Annette, I knew that I needed to decide how to carve out a future for myself. I knew what I did *not* want to do. I was determined to avoid the life of a laborer or tradesman. The first step, then, was abundantly clear—I would need a college education. Living only a few miles from Purdue, it was my logical choice for a university.

God bless our government for approving the G.I. Bill. I have no idea how many took advantage of it to further their education, but the beneficial impact on our lives could never be calculated. Nor will I ever know whether I would have gotten my B.A. without the G.I. Bill. Not only was my tuition paid, but also, I received a monthly check for a whopping $75!

As a generalization, I have never liked "bigness." Nature is an exception—mountains, sky, rivers, etc. Consequently, I was somewhat overwhelmed by the size of Purdue University. It was *many* times larger, more populated and more complete than the entire town where I was born. The enrollment (a *high* percentage of G.I. Joes) must have been about sixteen gazillion. I stayed for but one semester. During that time, I added a Chemistry course to my list of "dislikes." I enjoyed courses that required reasoning and logic. You can't reason with formulae.

The best part of my Purdue experience was not in academia, but in the field of entertainment. I acted in "Op of My Thumb," "A Family Portrait" and "A Night At an Inn." The stage performances were overshadowed by my return to singing with a band. This time, it was truly a "big" band (a rare exception to my distaste for bigness).

On a bulletin board announcement, I read that the newly formed Maury Gorden band was to hold auditions for a male and a female singer. Despite my minimal experience, I was confident that I would be hired.

I must admit to wiping beads of perspiration off my forehead as I stood in the bandstand and shook sweaty hands with Mr. Gorden (he immediately wiped his hand on his pants, but didn't seem repulsed—as I thought he might).

All during my military career, I had listened to the latest songs and learned most of the words. As my confidence grew, Mr. G. asked, "What do you do best, Frank—ballads, jive, jazz—what?" I boldly replied, "All of the above, but I prefer ballads—love songs." "How about doing "All or Nothing at All"?" he asked. I said, "Great." Not only did I know it well, but the title was appropriate. This could make or break my chances. But then came a blow. He asked, "What key, Frank?" Not knowing, I tried to cover up by smiling and saying, "Same as the other Frank." Showing more patience than I had a right to expect, he turned to the band and shouted, "Key of G, boys." Happily, it went well. I did my best Sinatra interpretation. To see how I could handle an upbeat tempo, he next had me do "Kalamazoo." During all of this, I was aware of an attractive girl observing me from a chair next to the bandstand. She was apparently there to audition for the "girl singer" spot, because Maury called to her. "Elaine, how about you and Frank doing a "Green Eyes" duet?" Beaming with joy, she almost *ran* to join me at the microphone.

Of the several thrills I've had in my life, this certainly qualified as one of them. All of a sudden I was Bob Eberle and she was Helen O'Connell. What a magical moment! It was as though we'd gone through a dozen practice sessions. Timing and rhythm were flawless. She must have heard "Green Eyes" as often as I had. As we did the coda—"make my dreams come true"— Maury did just that. He strode up to us, and, with a broad grin, put one hand on Elaine's shoulder and one on mine. Turning to the band, he said, "Well, gang, what do you think?" We nearly jumped for joy as they responded in unison, "Yeah, man," as the drummer gave a "boom dada boom." I hadn't been so euphoric since Jean Stokes pinned my wings on my tunic.

We held a number of practice sessions and performed at several different locations before I left Purdue. Whether doing a solo or a duet, our association was muy simpatico—but, like all good things, it was not to last. Another college beckoned—a *small*, private all male college only twenty-five miles from home. It was Wabash College. The faculty (and many others) proudly referred to it as "The Harvard of the Midwest." I had read about it and talked to others of its high standards. Its size (only five hundred men at the time), its location and its reputation were just what I had hoped for in a college. Although Purdue was (is) an excellent school, engineering and other technical disciplines were its primary thrust and focus. My interests were geared more for a liberal arts education (fortunately, the word "liberal" had no socio-political implications at the time).

Getting a transfer wasn't easy, but it certainly was worth the effort. Not only did it provide the foundation for an *excellent* education, but also, I was accepted as a pledge into the Phi Delta Theta fraternity. Most of the fellows were from affluent families, but there was hardly a hint of snobbery. In fact, it was through the fraternity that I met a fellow who was also an ex-G.I. He had been in the "V-12," the Navy version of my Air Cadet program at Syracuse University. Our association was much like "The Odd Couple," with my friend as "Oscar" and me as "Felix." The similarity was essentially confined to our disparate attitudes and lifestyles.

His name was Robert C. Finucane. (The "C"? After fifty-six years of friendship, I *still* don't know, but he would fume when I called him "Clyde.") Why we were to become lifelong friends remains a mystery. The fact that we were both devout Catholics was perhaps the strongest cohesive force—initially. We were apples and oranges—both all right but very different. I was the rigid Germanic military perfectionist and Bob was maddeningly "Irish-casual."

To this day I cannot recall how or why we decided to rent an off-campus room together, but probably because we could share the expense. It would have cost at least twice as much to live at the fraternity house. I was glad to have someone to cut my expenses, but Bob was more concerned with being away from the fraternity house. Although most of the fellows were "great guys," he could never grasp the gung-ho, eager beaver achiever concept. Personally, I felt quite proud to be associated with an affluent crowd and to call myself a "Phi Delt." It took a bit of humility, but I considered myself fortunate in being able to pay my dues and get my meals by washing dishes and serving tables.

Shortly after joining the fraternity, Bob saw a "Room for Rent" sign in the window of an older two-story home very near the campus. At his suggestion, we decided to investigate. The room was on the second floor in front of the house. It had been rented to students before, so there were two desks, two chairs and adequate space. The landlady, Mrs. Miller, was a tough old biddy, but, after signing the agreement to rent, we saw little of her. The stairway to our room was isolated from the rest of the house. But, oh, the fury on Friday nights! Poor, Claude—Mr. Miller. When he came home with the week's paycheck, Mrs. Miller would lay into him in a fit of rage. The yelling was predictable and on schedule, but we never heard a word out of old Claude. But then, she was bigger than he. Wimpish and downtrodden, Claude, we deduced, would have been lost without his nagging wife. In a strange way, they needed each other.

Bob had made it abundantly clear that he was annoyed by my fastidiousness. I kept my shoes neatly aligned in the closet and buttoned my shirts on their hangers, just as we did in the service. My books stood at attention between their stiffly functional bookends. Bob, by contrast, had his belongings strewn helter-skelter about the room. When his pants did occasionally make it to a hanger, they were draped loosely, inviting every possible wrinkle. His idea of a clothes hamper was any open spot on the floor. Yet, he always managed to look all right, one reason being the expensive and handsome (wrinkle-free) sweaters that were his trademark. They elegantly masked the wrinkled shirts.

Our class schedules were, of course, different; consequently, one of us would often be in class while the other would be studying in our room. One afternoon I came home and found my books scattered all over the floor and my shoes in a pile. I wasn't terribly surprised. Bob was as irritated with fussiness as I was with carelessness. Strange as it seems, I didn't get angry. I merely set about putting things back in order. When Bob returned I said, "You made your point, Clyde, now, do you feel better?" He replied, "As a matter of fact, I do." He just had to get it out of his system. After that, there seemed to be a tacit truce. We not only learned to accept each other for what we were, but also, we learned the value of good-natured needling. I would call him "Bob the Slob" and he'd click his heels and give me a stiff "Heil, Hitler." Behind the jabs and parries, however, a deep respect and camaraderie was developing. It has never diminished.

Excitement reached a fever pitch when a fraternity dance was held. Girls had to be imported from far and beyond. The nearest college was in Greencastle, some miles away from Crawfordsville. I was always pantingly eager and Bob was ho hum about it. It was maddening. Bob was a carbon copy of Montgomery Clift, the black-haired, handsome movie star. He could have had any girl he wanted, while I, the overanxious one, went begging... Well, not exactly, but its almost axiomatic that most women are drawn to the casual, cool, hard-to-get men. Bob wasn't just "hard-to-get," he was unavailable. He preferred going back to his home in Chicago to attending a frat dance.

Annette and her mother had moved to a distant city. In God's plan, the timing was right. The ardor of our relationship had begun to diminish after I moved to Crawfordsville. But life without a girlfriend was, to me, an unthinkable existence. Enter Kay Harris.

Kay had been in one of my classes at Jefferson High before the war, and I recalled that she had had a suggestive aura of sensuality about her. I decided to call her one weekend and was somewhat surprised that she remembered me. I tingled at the sultry sound of her voice. To my happy amazement, she seemed excited to hear from me and agreed to see me the next evening. She was so much like Lauren Bacall in every way but height and hair color that, after hanging up, I found myself doing Bogey imitations... "Whaddaya shay, kid? Wanna boogie with Bogey?" Nah—it wouldn't work. Maybe she'd like me for the boyish guy that I was.

When she greeted me at the door the next evening, I couldn't have been more pleased. She was as I had remembered her. Jet-black hair, large smoldering eyes that were dark and wide-set, and an enigmatic smile. It was not the broad, joyful smile of innocence, but rather, a cool, sensual half-smile reinforcing the

Bacall similarity. She took my hand warmly as we exchanged the "how long has it beens," the "how've you beens," and the "good to see yous." She led me into the livingroom where I met her smiling mother. She was a quiet, unassuming and charming lady. When she eventually excused herself to leave the room, my heart sank as I realized that she had a deformed foot and walked with difficulty. Then it struck me—it was an uncanny déjà vu as I thought of Annette and her mother. Both Kay and Annette were short. Both lived at home, caring for their invalid, widowed mother. What was going on here? It was an eerie feeling that passed quickly.

We had but a few months of bliss when Kay gave me some depressing news. She had accepted an offer that was too good to refuse. She was to become head nurse at a Miami Beach clinic. I knew that she had not been very happy in her position as a hospital nurse, but never expected her to take a job that far away. She urged me to come down for a visit during Easter week—two months away. She said that, by then, she would know whether she enjoyed her job enough to stay in Florida. Her dream was that I could transfer to the U. of Miami. Despite having very little money and an uncertain future, I readily agreed to visit her in early April.

When I told Bob about the pending trip, he snapped, "You must be crazy! That's over 1,200 miles from here. How will you get there—hitch-hike?" "Whatever it takes," I replied with feigned insouciance. I would hop a freight, if necessary, but I opted for my usual rule-of-thumb. I was no stranger to hitchhiking. I had been "thumbing" my way to and from home on many weekends.

The period from late January to April took approximately three years. When I told my family of my plan, it was like, "What? Are you crazy or something?!" My brilliant and original retort was, "Love does funny things to you."

The day after classes were dismissed for the holiday week, I took my stuffed flight bag and hit the road. One of the Phi Delts who had a car drove me to the highway. In only a few minutes I got the first of *many* rides as I worked my way south. Kay had given me her address on Biscayne Boulevard, and a nice retired couple took me straight to her door.

We were thrilled to be together again. Kay had purchased a car, so we were soon seeing the sights. We were euphoric. And to think that, after boot camp in Mississippi years ago, I had never wanted to see *any* of the south again. Miami and its environs had a tantalizing tropical ambience about it. It was intoxicating. We drank it in with relish.

In trying to "do it all," I made an error that nearly cost me my life. We had decided to rent bicycles and cruise along the beach pathway. I had forgotten how deadly the sun was at that latitude. Kay was apparently more acclimated and prepared because the intensity of the sun didn't seem to bother her. I, however, soon found myself burning up, yet clammy, then light-headed. I felt faint and slipping away as I tried to tell Kay. When I woke I was back in my hotel room, lying on the bed with only my briefs on. My cherry-red body gleamed with some salve or ointment. I was getting the professional care of my own private nurse. Thanks be to God, Kay knew just what to do—and what *not* to do—for sunstroke. It wasn't long before I was on my feet again and enjoying the Moon over Miami (forget the sun!).

As the precious days rapidly melted away, our conversations grew increasingly serious. So much so, in fact, that I asked her to marry me. We loved each other, but there was an overwhelming problem—religious differences. She was a Protestant and I a Catholic. She was convinced that the Pope would be standing between us (in retrospect I say, "Thank God for the Pope!"). Strong disagreements—religious, political, ethnic, etc.—often kill an otherwise happy marriage. We knew that, and with deepest regret, we agreed that it was not meant to be. Crestfallen and dispirited, I packed my bag and slowly deposited it in Kay's car. The ride to the northbound highway was a blur—literally. I don't know how Kay did it. We both sat with tear-filled eyes. Once, she briefly glanced at me and said, "Frank, don't you think we could…?" She couldn't finish. She firmly grasped my hand as I stepped gloomily into a gentle rain. I didn't look as she sped away. Our song had ended but a melody would linger on. As time goes by, we'll know if we've done the right thing.

CHANGE PARTNERS

The break-up with Kay marked the beginning of an improved new life for me—although I was painfully unaware of it for some time after leaving her. One door had been closed to me, but another was about to be opened.

After my return to Wabash College, I felt a pronounced void in my life. Part of me just wasn't there anymore. I prayed for direction. I meditated upon my past. After considerable soul-searching, I reached a conclusion that was to dramatically change my life forever—and for the better. Upon reflection, I realized that there had always been a girl in my life, and an all-male college certainly didn't help in that area. The solution to my dilemma occurred to me as I pondered my options.

While in the Air Force, one of my assignments had taken me to an air base in Pueblo, Colorado. While there, I had met and dated a lovely Irish-Catholic girl—Margaret Connors. Also while at Pueblo, I had explored Colorado College in Colorado Springs. I was quite impressed but considered it financially out of my league and too far from home and loved ones. Now, however, the thought of a transfer to "C.C." had great appeal. It would provide at least three benefits: I would be near Margaret, C.C. had a Phi Delta house where I could work and live and, last but not least, C.C. was co-ed. I had kept up an irregular correspondence with Margaret and knew that she would applaud the idea. I wrote and told her of my plan. Her reply was immediate and enthusiastic. She stated that it would be a "dream come true."

The high scholastic standards set by Wabash actually served me well. C.C. required an overall B+ average to achieve a transfer in, and I had maintained such an average. The more I thought about it, the more excited I became, although I was very pleased with Wabash and proud to have been a student there. I was also quite fond of the Phi Delta Theta brothers, but felt confident that the C.C. group would be of comparable quality and stature.

My parents and family were predictably saddened and disappointed to learn of my decision, but hoped that Margaret would fill the void left by the loss of Annette and Kay. So did I.

In the spring of 1947, after considerable correspondence between Wabash and Colorado College, my transfer was approved. Since I wouldn't enter C.C. until September, I decided to move into the Pueblo YMCA, get a summer job and see whether sparks would again fly between Margaret and me.

Several things had attracted me to Margaret when we first got acquainted (through a church function). She was an attractive "Irish Colleen," she was a "good Catholic girl," I liked her family, and she had that essential trait—a good sense of humor. We kidded each other a lot. What I needed to learn more about was the depth of her character, the degree of her maturity and responsibility and just how we really felt about each other. Our relationship had been quite light-hearted and superficial. We were always laughing and joking, but we didn't really *know* each other.

I had not yet learned the wisdom of realistically lowering one's expectations; Margaret unwittingly helped me in that area. Time and distance had put a halo above my glowing recollection of her, but it faded like a wisp of smoke shortly after our happy reunion. My every attempt to be serious was met with shallow laughter and an evasive, diversionary comment. Margaret was a lovely girl—a lot of fun—but maturity and depth of character were clearly lacking.

My full-time summer job—delivering furniture for the Goldstein Furniture Company—left me exhausted most evenings; this gave me a logical excuse for tapering off the frequency of dates with Margaret. I also took a bus to Colorado Springs several weekends and stayed at the C.C. Phi Delt house since it was nearly unoccupied during the summer.

Margaret may have been obtuse, but she had enough awareness to sense a growing chasm in our relationship. Because of her inability—or unwillingness—to express her true feelings, I couldn't tell whether she experienced pain or mere neutral nonchalance when I finally left in the fall. I knew that I would miss her cheerful chatter, but was also eager to meet someone of real substance. We mutually agree to "keep in touch," and I was off to start an exciting new chapter in the continuing saga of my eventful life. Little did I know that my enrollment at Colorado College was to become the catalyst that would launch me into a new world of fulfillment and reward.

SEPTEMBER SONG

I can only imagine the frustrating quagmire I would have been in had it not been for the brothers at the Phi Delt house; they took me—and the other "new" Phis—under their collective wing and were an immense help with our orientation process in September. Mother Brusse, our housemother, provided considerable comfort and guidance during this adjustment period also.

The small-college atmosphere was exactly what I wanted and needed. There were scheduled afternoon "faculty teas" during which we would share snacks and a beverage-of-choice (non-alcoholic, of course) with our professors. Many lively, open and educational conversations probably produced more learning than did the lecture halls. It was not only exhilarating to "rub elbows" with brilliant (and friendly) academics, but it was also intellectually stimulating. I felt that I had found my niche—and it was comfortable.

Colorado College is an old and renowned liberal arts institution, having been established in 1874. The sprawling, tree-filled campus held many solid and imposing buildings of stone that stand firmly to this very day. Although it has maintained an excellent reputation for academic excellence, it was also considered a school for the country club set. Many of the 1,200 students came from "old money" families back east.* Ski resorts, a picturesque setting and exclusivity served as irresistible magnets. The influx of returning ex-G.I.s like myself injected a more mature ethos into the atmosphere, but the dignity and stature of old C.C. was never compromised. The "richness" was somewhat diluted by our being part of the mix, but the quality of the stalwart institution was not.

A fortuitous meeting with Dr. Blakely, the Psychology Department head, prompted me to switch from a major in English to a Psych. Major—a move I have never regretted. I found the subject fascinating and was soon serving as Laboratory Assistant to the department head. Dr. Blakely strongly urged me to wholeheartedly pursue a Ph.D. with the goal of becoming a psychiatrist. I felt honored and encouraged, but the good Lord had other plans for me—plans for which I will be eternally grateful.

Always the spotlight seeker, I did my share of stage production time, as I had done at Purdue. Stage plays,

*Two prominent alumni come to mind: Lynne Cheney, wife of Vice President Dick Cheney, and Helen Stevenson, niece of Adlai Stevenson.

singing "gigs"—we even had Saturday morning radio shows. Those were halcyon days indeed. Through such exhilarating functions, I met several attractive, wealthy, spirited and intelligent girls—mostly from the affluent suburbs north of Chicago. I especially remember—with pleasure—the girl who had a blue convertible. But for rain or snow, she always had her top down (providing considerable fodder for jokes by the ogling fellows). Although I dated several, all of whom were amenable and congenial, I never felt truly at ease. It was the same situation in high school when in the company of the "well off." I knew that I didn't belong, and they must have been aware of my discomfort. This condition may very well have been a motivating factor in my determination to succeed in each future endeavor. I wonder how many saw through my veneer of self-confidence. No matter, it served me well, for, by affecting and air of assurance, it eventually became genuine. I even achieved the rank of President of the C.C. Newman club.

This was an active socio-religious organization for Catholic students on campus. The C.C. founders were strongly Protestant. All students were required to attend frequent services in Shove Chapel—which was more like a towering European cathedral. Forced attendance was a source of considerable irritation for most Catholic students, so the Newman Club satisfied the need for a common bond. I don't know how I got to be its president, but what happened while in office was to (happily) change my life forever.

AT LAST

One of the members of the club was Mary Ann Volk, a student who also worked part-time in a department store. The young clothing buyer for the store, Anne Venie—a friend of Mary Ann's and a Catholic also—expressed an interest in attending Newman Club meetings. Since college-age non-students were permitted to join, the two girls came to the next meeting together.

I had come to recognize most of the members, so, when I saw a new face next to Mary Ann, I asked her to be introduced to the group. Anne was warmly accepted, and small wonder. She was cute and perky with an infectious, heart-warming smile and dark brown eyes that fairly danced. Her graceful carriage and charisma so impressed me that I had great difficulty in concentrating on the business at hand. I cut the meeting short—all too eager to meet this sparkling charmer. Mary Ann—a blond beauty in her own right—sensed my keen interest in Anne and tactfully made an excuse to leave us alone. Anne willingly agreed to join me in the Ratskeller—a student hangout—for coffee. Funny thing—neither of us liked coffee at the time, but it sounded more "mature" than a cherry coke.

The mutual interest was immediately apparent to each of us. Each answered question was a springboard to another until we knew a great deal about each other. The more I learned about Anne, the more enthused I became about developing our relationship. She seemed to feel the same way, but with more caution. Her strength of character shone through as she told me about the sudden death of her forty-one year old father only one month prior to our meeting. I could only imagine the trauma of this lovely, innocent eighteen-year-old daughter when she discovered her adored father lying dead on the kitchen floor. Tears welled in her eyes as she described the scene. She had idolized this kind and gentle man. His name, incidentally, was Francis, the same as mine.

I also learned that Anne was an only child who longed for brothers and sisters. Her mother had explained the physical impossibility of this, so it's no wonder that she was ecstatic when I told her that I had *six sisters* and *four brothers*! She went on to explain that she and her mother, Eleanor, lived in a small upstairs apartment not far from the campus. Eleanor had been used to a life of relative luxury. She had never held a job of any sort, but now had no other choice. Consequently, both she and Anne found work in town. Eleanor worked in a clothing store and Anne, despite her lack of experience (and much to her credit) soon became a clothing buyer in Kaufman's Department Store—Colorado Springs' largest at the time. She had shown incredible strength in the face of adversity—as had Eleanor. I admired not only her spunkiness, but also her tenderness, her compassion—everything I learned or assumed about her. Although I was five years her senior, her engaging maturity easily put us on a par.

Our minds were so focused on learning more and more about each other that the clerk finally had to tap me on the shoulder and repeat, "It's time to close." I looked up with astonishment and said, "But we just got here!" Then, to Anne, I added, "Didn't we?" Her eyes twinkled as she smiled and replied, "It certainly seems like it to me."

As I walked her home, we continued our lively conversation. I soon sensed a bit of melancholy in her voice, however. She became quiet as we approached her door. There was even reluctance as I took her hand to say "goodnight." Any thought I had of attempting a parting kiss was quickly dismissed. She did—with some hesitancy—agree to see me again the next week. It was to be on my twenty-fourth birthday (I didn't tell her this, for fear it might put her in an embarrassing position).

As I returned to the Phi Delt house, I was filled with convoluted and conflicting thoughts and feelings. I had ridden the emotional roller coaster at varying levels of thrill and thrall many times before—Annette, Kay, the "Magnificent Seven" and others. Did I dare tempt fate yet again? What if I had misread the signals? Maybe Anne was just sweet and lovely to every guy she met. But, no—there had been a clear and genuine attraction. We had both felt the magnetic strength of it. It was undeniable. Whey then, the sudden change in her demeanor? Had she been "burned" in the past? Did she fear commitment? Was she just a temptress? No! I could never believe that! I *had* to find the answers and could hardly wait to see her again.

It was a pain/thrill kind of week. The waiting and wondering were agony, but the anticipation was ecstasy. I recall a fellow Phi—Tom Backus—asking, "What gives, Frank? You're mind's a hundred miles away." "About six blocks is more like it," I answered. "I met the girl I'm going to marry and she lives in an apartment near here. We have a date Saturday night." With a tone of incredulity, Tom asked, "You're kidding. What about Carol and Jeanette and Barbara? And, besides, how can you already be so sure about what's-her-name?" "Her name is Anne and, after our conversation, I feel I've known her forever—she's everything I've ever dreamed of—and then some. If my prayers are answered, Carol and the rest are history."

After I explained how we had met, what we had in common, what I had learned (and inferred) about

Anne, Tom asked, "So when do I meet this dream-girl, this queen?" "First, I make my case, then, who knows, she may give you an audience if you play your cards right," I blithely replied.

Aware of my plan to take Anne to the Patty Jewett Country Club the night of my birthday, tricky Tom alerted his brother Phis and they agreed to give me a surprise party—not knowing whether I would be pleased or furious with them. They arrived ahead of us, of course, and, as Anne and I stepped into the main dining hall, we were greeted with a rousing "Happy Birthday" song. Our faces must have been as red as the roses Tom had arranged for our table. I couldn't have been more proud—and "Queen Anne" (as Tom called her) handled it with the grace, poise and charm that I might have expected of her. She won the hearts of all in the room—and I was the envy of each Phi. As we waited for dinner to be served Tom came to our table and asked, "Do I get my audience with the queen now?" With a long-suffering sigh, I stood and said, "Anne, I'm honor-bound to intro-duce you to one crazy guy—Tom Backus." With his customary panache, Tom doffed an imaginary hat, swung his arm in a wide arc and bowed in courtly fashion, then softly kissed Anne's hand. I said, "You clown! So you're the court jester. Are you respon-sible for all this?" "I must plead guilty, your highness. Just mete out my just desserts." "No dessert for you, fella—just bring some to Anne and me—What'll you have, Anne?" "I'll have a fudge sundae—but don't you think Tom should have some humble pie?" That did it. She had again risen to the occasion and aced Tom. He loved her for it. So did I.

After dinner, I asked Anne if she would come with me to the clubhouse baby grand piano. With a quizzical smile she said, "Now, don't tell me you play piano!" Wryly, I said, "Oh, just a little." Trying to appear nonchalant and competent, I sat down at the keyboard and played as much of "Clair de Lune" as I could, then I stood and casually said, "I'm too rusty on the rest of it"—but I had played just enough to be convincing. "I'm in love with you" was what I read in her eyes. What she didn't know was that I had been practicing on the college music department's piano for days!

The evening—our first *real* date—was a smashing success. One of the Phis had loaned me his car for my birthday, so I could not recall experiencing a more intoxicating feeling as I drove Anne to her door. Before saying goodnight, however, I sensed the same gloom in Anne that I had felt before. This time, however, I was determined to find the reason. I blurted out, "Anne, I've seen that look before. You know that I love you, but something's wrong; what is it?" Misty-eyed, she struggled to speak. "I don't know what to do. I'm unofficially engaged. Bob is overseas in the army. He *did* say it was alright for me to have an occasional date, though. I *really* intended to marry him—but now—I have such strong feelings for you, Frank. I just *can't* hurt Bob. What in the world will I do?" "Kiss me," I whispered, "then let's talk about it." After considerable discussion, we decided to pray for guidance—and—to see each other again—soon—to "work things out." At that point, the porch light flashed off and on several times. Startled, Anne asked, "Oh! What time is it?" I squinted at my watch. "It's nearly two o'clock—no wonder your mother's concerned." I saw her to the door, kissed her lightly and left—eager for our next date. The problem *had* to be resolved and I was determined not to lose her.

Eventually Anne softened enough to introduce me to her mother. Eleanor was tall, dignified and stately, with a regal bearing. Irish through and through, however. I felt that there lurked a wry sense of humor in her make-up, although she was understandably cautious and reserved. After all, she fully expected the handsome, debonair and potentially successful Bob Cordry to become her son-in-law, then along comes this jobless, career-less, nearly penniless fellow to upset the applecart. A mixture of emotions hovered about each one of us. Anne wanted to be loyal to Bob, yet had "strong feelings" for me. I knew that I loved Anne, but felt like a cad and an interloper. We decided to meet less frequently to see what happened. Actually, the separation merely served to intensify my desire to be with her. Her sense of honor and loyalty wouldn't let her openly admit it, but I felt certain that she preferred me to Bob—or was it just wishful thinking?

I'LL REMEMBER APRIL

❧❦❧

Just before Easter, Anne invited me to have brunch with her and Eleanor after Sunday Mass. "Aha! I'm making progress," I thought. It worked out beautifully. As I stood next to her while she fried eggs in their tiny kitchen, I wondered if she had the same fantasy of wedded bliss that I did. I even got the feeling that Eleanor wouldn't mind having me for a son-in-law.

Soon after that joyous day, I invited Anne to a formal fraternity dance at Cheyenne Mountain Lodge. She seemed delighted. Tom had just bought a new sedan and offered to take us with him and his date. When we arrived at Anne's apartment I rang the doorbell and was promptly greeted by an ever more lovely Anne—striking in a beautiful evening gown. I pinned a corsage on her shoulder and we joined Tom and Nancy. When Tom saw Anne looking so stunning, he blurted out, "Wow!" I couldn't see Nancy's face, but could only imagine her cool reaction.

We were soon dancing on clouds—both figuratively and literally. The lodge was situated at an elevation of over seven thousand feet, and it was hidden in clouds. The ambience—dimly lighted chandeliers; a huge fireplace; a spacious dance floor with an excellent orchestra—made us feel "light-headed," the altitude notwithstanding. Even before the thrill of the evening had begun, I had firmly decided that I would propose to Anne before the night was over. On the dance floor I said, "You gotta love a guy who hasn't stepped on your toes all evening." Her shining eyes twinkled as she sidestepped the comment by saying playfully, "That's only because I'm one step ahead of you." She danced like (and resembled) Ann Miller.

After the dance, Tom brought the car up to the entrance as we shivered in foggy, cold mountain air. Anne squeezed my hand as we entered the car and, from the dome-light, I could see a worried look on her face—a look that I shared. The heavy fog put visibility at close to zero. Our intrepid driver was not only unfazed by it, but was soon careening down the steep, serpentine mountain road. We were silently petrified. Nancy finally pleaded, "Can't you slow down, Tom?" In his breezy way, he shot back, "Hey! I'm just giving Frank some opportunity corners." "Don't do me any favors, Tom. Just get us down in one piece!" I roared.

During the entire terrifying descent, Anne not only squeezed my hand, but also clung to my arm as the car swayed around the curves and hairpin turns. The close body contact was such that we were soon in an embrace—laced with both ardor and fear. I must admit that I enjoyed each "opportunity corner."

When we finally reached flat land and were on a straight course, my mouth went dry and my pulse raced. My entire future was at stake. It was "do or die" and I felt it might be the latter. I asked Tom to increase the volume of the radio music (to muffle my words), then in a state of near panic, I stammered, "Anne—" Just then we passed under a streetlight and I saw the blending of anxiety and expectancy in her sparkling eyes. "Anne—will you m—m—Will you be my—" "Your *wife*?" she glowingly asked. With a broad, warm smile, she eagerly uttered the most eloquent, life-defining words I had ever heard. "Yes, *yes*! I *will*!" To adequately describe my reaction—picture someone who has just won a multi-million dollar jackpot. I could *not* have been happier. When Tom heard, "I will!" he shot back, "You will *what*, Anne?" Before she could reply, I chimed in, "She will change her name to mine, Nosey." "You must be nuts, Anne; who wants a name like Balen-whatever?" he gruffly joked. Then, in unison, he and Nancy bellowed, "*Congratulations*! Let's celebrate!" And we were off to the A&W drive-in (bear in mind that this was in the "good old days" of clean, wholesome fun). The root beer could have been 100 proof alcohol, to judge from our euphoric, dizzy state.

On the way home, Anne made an interesting revelation. She told me that the defining moment—the moment that she really *knew* that she wanted to marry me—was when I stood next to her as she fried eggs that Easter Sunday morning. Love is funny that way. "What about Bob?" I gently asked. With downcast eyes she replied, "I'll write to him tomorrow." "Good!" I said, "Before you change your mind!" She laughed, and then said, "Never!"

It was late when we arrived at Anne's place, but I knew that her mother would be waiting up for her. I rather suspect that she wasn't too surprised to learn that Bob Cordry was *not* to become her son-in-law.

There would be little sleep for Anne and me that night. Our minds overflowed with thoughts and dreams of a wondrous, happy life together. Surely, Camelot would be just around the corner.

GET ME TO THE CHURCH ON TIME

A nne's mother owned a La Salle sedan and, with my being considered almost part of the family, I was given free rein to drive it. We traveled to many points of interest and enjoyed mountain picnics and campfires. Eleanor accompanied us nearly *everywhere*. She was such a good sport and such fun to be with, however, that I didn't mind at all. I was convinced—and rightly so—that she would be an excellent mother-in-law, far from the stereotypical nag. That being the case, the old "mother-in-law" jokes just didn't fit.

Thoughts of our future together enthused us beyond description, but the pinnacle of joy was provided by the brother Phis. They left the campus at night to serenade us as I presented my fraternity pin to Anne as we stood on her doorstep. "Pinning" is a solemn and moving occasion, but serenading the couple off-campus was *unprecedented* (and against fraternity rules and regulations). My beaming pride was matched only by the ecstasy Anne felt. Being crowned Miss America might have given her a greater thrill, but I don't think anything else would have.

After I attached the "sword and shield" pin (which bore a small diamond*) to Anne's sweater, and at the end of the serenade*, I heard someone—probably Tom—shout, "You may now kiss the bride-to-be!" I complied. After all, who was I to defy a Phi?

The months following the pinning were filled with the excitement of planning and preparing for the wedding. So eager was I that I decided to take summer classes, receive my B.A. in January and forego the June graduation ceremony. We had agreed to return to Anne's hometown parish for the wedding. It was to be held at St. Agnes church in Springfield, Missouri on January 24.

Patience is a virtue foreign to my temperament. When the war broke out, I could not wait to enlist, so I attended summer school in order to graduate mid-term. Of course, that meant missing the graduation ceremony. Nor did I wear a cap and gown at college graduation. At least I had my priorities in order. Now my patience was again being tested as the days, weeks

---

*The serenade song is entitled, "Tell Me Why She Wears His Pin."

and months dragged along. The waiting was even worse than the months before getting my wings.

When January *did* finally arrive, it brought with it a flurry of activity. Plans for packing the possessions of the three of us, plans for the trip to Missouri, plans for the wedding itself—Fortunately, Anne was (and *is*) a logistics expert by nature, consequently the move went like clockwork.

Colorado College had been an excellent school and the Phi Delts were a great bunch, but as we left beautiful Colorado Springs, our thoughts and feelings were fully and happily focused on the wedding and on the joyous life that lay ahead of us.

The ride to Springfield was carefree and trouble-free. The old La Salle performed well despite its heavy cargo in the trunk and most of the rear seat and floor. The days that followed our arrival were anything but uneventful, however. I could never have imagined the complexity, confusion and emotion that were all part of preparations for a wedding. Fortunately, Anne and Eleanor had plenty of help and moral support. Anne had attended both St. Agnes High and St. Jane de Chantal Academy in Springfield, so her old friends and classmates were itching to see the fellow who replaced Bob Cordry as her fiancé. They knew that Bob and Anne had been a serious item before Anne left for Colorado for her father's health. How strange the twists and turns in life. Anne had a scholarship to Webster Grove, an excellent college—but some idiot doctor had urged her father to move to Colorado for his health. The move killed him. I moved to Colorado to rekindle the flame with Margaret Connors—that died. I met and courted Anne, and her plans to marry Bob died. Yet, it all added up to a re-birth—and our vows were to be the midwife.

After all of the planning, work and love that went into the ceremony, the wedding came *very* close to being postponed!

The night before the wedding, as I was loading our "belongings" into the trunk of the car, I doubled over in *great* pain. I dropped the luggage and staggered to the house (I was staying with Anne's uncle and aunt and Anne stayed with her grandparents). Steve and Betty recognized the problem—appendicitis. Our only hope was the beneficial effects of ice packs throughout the night. Thanks to their prompt attention the pain reduced dramatically. That, coupled with the mega-doses of premarital adrenalin, carried me through miraculously. I met my bride with a frozen (right) side.

Weather predictions for the morning of January 24, 1950, could hardly have been worse. Freezing rain, hail, a mixture of snow and high winds. We all prayed fervently for a reprieve—and we got it! It was a beautiful, crisp morning—breezy, but not a gale.

Although a dream-come-true, the wedding itself was not quite what I had hoped for. I had wanted my best friend, Bob Finucane, to be my best man, and wanted my parents (if not even more family members) to attend. But, with the isolated exception of our blessed grace period, all of the Midwest weather was so bad that travel was nearly impossible. Anne's uncle, Steve Schneider, became my best man and I would not see my own family or Bob until several days later. The ceremony was beautiful, as was the bride and the participants (especially Peggy, our little flower girl). But then, after a brunch and a reception at the farm of Anne's Aunt Dedie, the delayed storm arrived. As we waved goodbye, it was not just to the well-wishers, but to all semblance of fair weather. Anne remarked that she wasn't sure that "Stormy Weather" would continue to be one of her favorite songs. Driving conditions were hazardous, but we felt invincible and weathered the storm nicely until we stopped for the night in a small town in southern Indiana.

It was, indeed, "a dark and stormy night" as we saw the fuzzy lights of a motel. The blurred sign said, "Sail Inn." The rain was torrential, but it didn't dampen our euphoric spirits. It took some time to rouse the innkeeper but when we did, the sleepy-eyed fellow brusquely gave us a key to number three and wryly said, "Good luck—just settle up in the mornin'." We soon discovered what he meant by "good luck." The deluge was such that water had come up to the door's threshold. We laughed about it and I told Anne that I was glad she was a good swimmer. We quickly placed the luggage on the vinyl floor—there were no racks—and removed out rain-soaked coats. We had barely crawled under the bedcovers when Anne sat up and, with a warning tone said, "Listen!" The sound we heard was similar to that of a small, babbling brook. As I turned on the bedside table lamp, what we saw startled us, but we laughed at the incident. As a "going away" gift, I had given Anne a sturdy, Samsonite cosmetic/personal care case (about 14"x10"x8"). We now saw it slowly floating toward the bathroom, as the water slithered under the entry door. As Anne tried to retrieve it, I sloshed my way to the other luggage and managed to stack it atop the lone dresser. To the "Sail Inn's" credit, the towels were clean and dry and the wall-heater worked. We thanked God for both.

By morning the rain had stopped and the water on the floor had receded. Making no complaint to the sullen innkeeper, we dutifully paid our bill and were off to Lafayette, where my family eagerly awaited our arrival.

We had no illusions about having a real honeymoon. Our meager funds were fast disappearing, so the three-day trip would have to suffice.

MOONLIGHT ON THE WABASH

A s it did on the morning of our wedding, the sky again cleared beautifully for the final leg of our journey. After lunch at a quaint colonial restaurant in Indianapolis, I was surprised and disappointed to find that we had a grand total of only fifty dollars left—this, despite our having spent our money on nothing frivolous. We were blissfully untroubled, however, and confident that we could easily get by until my first paycheck from General Telephone Company. Love is apparently not only blind, but also lives in denial—as we were to soon discover.

I don't recall how many of my family comprised the "welcoming committee," but there were enough to please us immensely—especially Anne. My plump and jolly mother immediately took her into her loving arms and gave her a bear hug—the likes of which

Anne had never felt. To this day, she laughs as she recalls that warm and wonderful moment. There was *no* doubt that my parents were more than delighted to find that their number two son had married such a marvelous girl. It was immediately apparent to all of the assembled that Anne would become a brilliant star in the Balensiefer galaxy. Her warmth, charm and cheerful perkiness were welcomed with (literally) open arms by all. Her cultured bearing of poise and grace belied her down-to-earth, dig-in attitude.

After the sumptuous, delicious welcoming dinner, and despite my sisters' protests, Anne began gathering the plates and utensils. The protests were useless against her Irish determination. My outspoken sister, Toots, finally said, "Hey, let her work! She *is* part of the family now." They all laughed and my emotional mother cried as, with dishtowel in hand, she gave Anne another bear hug. It was a proud moment as I realized even more fully what a treasure God had granted me—*and* my family.

Some time before our wedding, we had (with the help of my family) made arrangements to rent an upstairs apartment in South Lafayette. Having arrived in town on a Friday, we wasted no time and were moved in by Sunday afternoon. Our euphoric state was enhanced by the anticipation of my new career starting the next day. We couldn't have been happier, but I was, of course, a bit nervous about starting my new job. Anne was understandably curious about her new surroundings, so we decided to drive around and "see the sights"—*and* soothe our nerves.

During our courtship, I had often touted the beauty and wonder of the broad and fabled Wabash River that divided Lafayette and West Lafayette. Anne had learned some of the words to "Back Home Again in Indiana" and was charmed by the line, "How I dream about the moonlight on the Wabash, as I long for my Indiana home." I was pleased, then, when she eagerly urged me to take her to the river she had heard so much about. It was late in the day and the sky was overcast—not a good time to see the sun sparkling little gems on the dancing river that I recalled from years gone by. I was soon painfully reminded that time and distance can blur and embellish harsh realities.

Traffic was not a major problem in 1950, especially on a Sunday evening. We parked the car and walked out on the Fourth Street bridge. We stared in disbelief at the muddy, colorless torrent below. Anne tried valiantly to hide her disappointment, but finally looked into my eyes, shook her head slowly and, in a tone of astonishment said, "*This* is what you've been raving about!? This—this muddy stream? And—and where's the romantic moonlight you talked about? Huh!?" All during her tirade, she smiled through gritted teeth while giving me several fake body blows. In ducking her "blows," I caught sight of another couple on the other side of the bridge. They stopped and stared, not knowing what to do. I quickly subdued my cute "attacker" and took her in my arms. We turned, and smiling broadly at the perplexed couple, waved while I shouted, "It's okay. She was only kidding!" Then, turning my face to hers, I frowned and said, "At least I *think* she was." At that, we both laughed heartily. As I plaintively sang, "...How I dream about the moonlight on the Wabash..." the playful pummeling began anew. I admired Anne for the joking way she handled this minor disappointment. I was soon to learn more about her ability to deal with adversity.

We were thrilled with our apartment. The property had an abundance of elm, oak, sycamore and evergreen trees. The deciduous trees were, of course, barren in January, but the cedar, pine and fir held promise of Christmas-card beauty with the next snow. We had our private entrance to the flat by means of an outside staircase. The privacy it afforded would prove to be to our considerable benefit.

There were two bedrooms (Anne's mother would soon move in), a livingroom, a kitchen with dinette and a large bathroom. The cozy pinewood dinette booth also served as our "conference table." We were to hold many discussions there—some serious and angst-laden; some lighthearted and cheerful.

On that Sunday night—our first in the flat—I slept fitfully. When I would look at Anne in the dim nightlight, I could see a hint of a blissful smile. To her, God was in His Heaven and all was right with the world. I had difficulty calming the butterflies in my stomach.

The thought of my joining the Personnel Department of a huge corporation such as General Telephone was both disquieting and stimulating. I had to fight off a case of the "what-ifs." When morning came, however, Anne's blithe spirit and positive attitude soon had me convinced that all would go well on my first day on the job. She waved goodbye to me as I backed the car out of the driveway and I threw a kiss, shouting, "Look out world, here I come!"

⚘

The foyer of the telephone company was somewhat austere, but the attractive young receptionist added the needed warmth to the atmosphere. There was apparently no reason for me to explain why I was there. I had barely mentioned my name when the girl's welcoming smile revealed an almost imperceptible strain as she professionally intoned, "Oh, yes. Then Mr. Chillburn is the person you'll need to see. He's our Personnel Director. Have a seat while I tell him you're here." Although *what* she said was normal and standard protocol, *how* she said it made me a bit uneasy. And why had she left her desk to quietly disappear down the hall when she could have used the intercom? The few minutes of her absence served to increase my anxiety. When she finally reappeared, with averted eyes she spoke through an affected smile, "Mr. Chillburn will see you now. Just follow me." "Who wouldn't," I was tempted to say, as her provocative, black-stockinged legs undulated before me over the lush green carpet. I couldn't quite discern the subtle change in her general demeanor, but a touch of sadness was what I saw in the brief glimpse and averted eyes. My real concern, however, was the impression I would make on the Director of Personnel. Hair combed? Shoes shined? Tie and suit conservative enough? Youthful enthusiasm tempered with a mature bearing? With computer-like speed, the "do's and don'ts" of making a good impression clicked swiftly through my spinning brain. Despite my careful and thorough preparation for this moment, I had to make a concerted effort to calm the butterflies.

As I approached his impressive mahogany desk, I assumed that the man behind it would be my boss. He was tall and slender and impeccably dressed in a dark, flannel suit and a regimental striped tie. He was graying at the temples and had piercing eyes. His expression was not what I expected, however. There seemed to be an odd mixture of surprise, confusion and possibly a hint of vexation in his narrowed eyes and half-smile. As we shook hands, I wondered if he felt that moisture on mine. After a brief mutual "Good morning," his first words were not the usual, "Welcome aboard," but rather, "Didn't you get my letter?" The butterflies went wild as the implication hit me. "No sir—but I left Colorado on January 15th—perhaps…" "It went out the 14th—sorry we didn't get to you in time." His tone was actually laced with sympathy. "In *time*?" I asked—as if the explanation was needed. "I really hate to tell you this Mr. Balensiefer (one rarely used first names in a business setting back then), but the position you were to fill was eliminated by the powers that be. Budget crunch, strikes, union problems—you know." No, I *didn't* know—but what could I say? Seeing my world crumbling down around me, I could only gulp and murmur, "This is quite a shock. My wife and I…" Then I remembered one of the primary tenets of leaving a good impression—Don't whine or give a sob story. I then asked a politely, "Would there be an alternative position in the company now, or in the near future?" His head was slowly shaking a "no" before the end of the question. With an ever-so-slight hint of apology, he intoned, "Sorry, but there's an indefinite moratorium on hiring. It's a bad time right now." "I'm sorry, too, Mr. Chillburn, but I can see that it's beyond your control. Too bad the recruiter didn't know about this when he offered me the position before I graduated." At this, he stood up and, with a note of finality, stated rather firmly, "Things happen fast in a corporation like ours." Then, with a somewhat patronizing and dismissive pat on my back, he said, "I'm sure you'll do well wherever you go. Anyone who can measure up to General Telephone standards has a lot going for him. Good luck to you." My parting handshake must have felt feeble, because the rest of me was certainly weak and deflated.

As I passed through the lobby, the receptionist, with a pained expression and fleeting eye contact, spoke to me—just above a whisper—"I'm so sorry." I smiled—"Thanks. I would have liked it here." It was *not* a good way to start the day—or a new life. How would Anne react to this terrible news? What would we do for income? How could I break it to her? Her would-be Junior Executive was just another unemployed guy with a seemingly worthless diploma.

When I returned to the apartment, Anne was understandably surprised, but the dour look on my face told her the story. She said, "You didn't get the job!?" It was more a statement than a question. After explaining the details, I quickly added—with as much enthusiasm as I could muster, "I'll get another job, and I'll bet I'll be working tomorrow. I bought a newspaper. There'll be something in the classified ads." She tried to smile bravely, but the worry was obvious. I tilted her chin up, smiled and said, "Hey, Spunky—we'll pull through—W.P.T., remember?" (I had used this during our courtship when funds were almost gone). Her eyes were moist as she replied, "You bet! And I know we will—but..." I put my finger to her lips and said hopefully, "Let's look at the ads." We did, and were sorely disappointed at the dearth of opportunities. The only opening that seemed worth pursuing was in insurance sales. It held no appeal to me, but it was the only possibility. The ad read, "Start at Once! No experience necessary." The "at once" did it. Time was not on our side.

As I left to begin my job search the next morning, Anne's spunk came through clearly as she said, "Don't worry, we have peanut butter and we can make pancakes. W.P.T. for sure!" With forced alacrity, I said, "I'll be on someone's payroll by tonight. Meanwhile,

186

though, it wouldn't hurt to look up the name of the patron saint of job hunters." She laughed as I drove away. Neither of us wanted to worry the other, but we both knew that the treasured fifty dollars couldn't last very long.

***

The bubbly and pert gum-chewing receptionist at the insurance office handed me a clipboard and an application form. The questions on the form were quite elementary. In fact, I got the impression that, if you were willing and able to sell insurance, little else mattered.

When Miss Bubbly gave my completed form to the agent, he gave it a two-second review, then bounced out of his chair with an outstretched hand. It was apparent that he couldn't care less about my credentials. He could see that I was about 25, clean-cut, well dressed and friendly—the only requisites he cared about. I was prepared to define my qualifications but found that he was eagerly extolling the benefits of selling health insurance. After his exuberant "you can go to the moon" oration, with a gleaming, toothy smile, he asked, "How about it, Frank (not "Mr. Balensiefer")? Want to play on our team?" Before I could reply, he said, "If you can be here tomorrow morning, I'll take you out and get your feet wet—ha ha." I was in no position to say, "Let me think about it." In his discourse, he had guaranteed a weekly "draw against commission." A draw meant cash-in-hand.

I would deal with the commission part of it later. "What time should I be here?" I found myself sounding eager. "Good man, Frank! I'll see you at o-nine hundred (implying, I guess, that he, too, had been in military service). Then I heard the words I had so hoped to hear from Mr. Chillburn—"Welcome aboard!" (Maybe he'd been in the Navy?)

When I gave Anne the good news, she threw her arms around my neck and gleefully shouted, "I *knew* you'd get it! Let's celebrate!" My first draw was a week (or two, if they withheld the first week) away, so we knew we couldn't afford to get to frivolous. "Can our budget allow a movie and popcorn?" I asked. Later, sitting in the balcony of the Mars Theater, Anne squeezed my hand and, in a stage whisper, said, "Is this Heaven or what!?" I resisted a pun on the altitude of the balcony. It was, indeed, a heady moment. Our cares could wait. It was popcorn time in la la land.

David Greenback, the insurance agent, was heavily pumping my hand at "0900" the next morning. We were promptly off to pursue a "lead." Initially, each salesman was given a 3x5 card for each prospective customer, but was required to develop his owns leads after the training period. There were "cold" leads and "hot" leads (the latter being rare, I soon discovered). David's attitude was the epitome of enthusiastic optimism. I was supposed (and expected) to be infected by it. Unfortunately, I found it to be smothering overkill. His saccharine glad-handing notwithstanding, I was determined to do my best to learn his sales techniques, which were apparently successful in the "long haul."

The response to most of our calls was usually colder than the leads themselves. Most would agree that health insurance was a good thing, but few were willing to pay for it. According to David, it was not uncommon to have eight out of ten of the prospects give a negative response—but that meant a twenty percent success ratio. Over time, it could be profitable.

By the end of the day, I was emotionally drained and almost overcome with doubt. I put on a happy face and told Anne that it hadn't been bad at all—that it would just take time to adapt to a different world. The sales field was still foreign to me. Her pancake supper helped take the edge off my anxiety. Tomorrow would be better...but it wasn't. I was too sensitive for the hard knocks that came with selling. You needed the hide of an elephant, but mine was that of a newborn baby. Nevertheless, I pressed on. Day after day I rang doorbells and made phone calls. Once in a while I would sell a health insurance policy. When I did, I was as happy to know that I had provided needed protection for the family as I was to earn my commission.

It didn't take long for me to realize that I could never be another David Greenback. I simply could *not* pressure people. When a prospect said he couldn't afford the premium, I could only sympathize and empathize.

Being "in the field" most of the day provided opportunities to consider my options. I did a fair job of hiding my angst from Anne while I covertly scanned the "help wanted" ads. It wasn't long before I saw an ad for a "floor salesman" at the local Sears-Roebuck & Co. appliance department. It, too, offered a draw against commission, but it would be inside sales—not a door-to-door arrangement. It also offered profit sharing and other benefits. I applied, was hired "on the spot" and rushed home to tell Anne. I found that she hadn't been fooled at all. She had sensed my frustration and disappointment but decided to give me the time and space to work things out. She shared my relief and joy, but asked, "How will David react to your quitting?" "They apparently have a high turnover rate, so I doubt he'll be surprised. He's no dummy. I'm sure he could tell that I was too thin-skinned to last in that pressure-cooker environment." Sure enough—when I gave my notice, David smiled broadly and said, "Hey, no need to apologize. We're not all made to like the rough and tumble. Me—I thrive on it. Good luck anyway, Frank. You'll do well wherever you go." (Where had I heard *that* before?)

⌑

Selling washers, dryers, stoves and refrigerators was a snap compared to insurance sales. Not only were these *tangible* products, but also, customers came to *me* instead of my beating the bushes in search of them. With the good reputation of Sears products, they were at least half sold before they walked through the door.

I adapted readily and did well for over a year, until, for a variety of complex reasons, we could not get enough appliances to supply the need. The city was burgeoning and supply versus demand became a serious problem. The only surplus was in salesmen. Seniority came into play. I could see the handwriting on the wall. The glow of a bright future was muted by the harsh reality. I was the "newest" employee in the department, so it came as no surprise when I heard the dreaded, "We hate to lose you" parting phrase. I was given two weeks' notice.

After a predictable expression of sympathy and compassion, Anne cryptically asked, "Are you ready for more bad news?" She then told me that our landlady, Mrs. Schaeffer, had just told her that she needed the flat for her son and his wife—that we would have to leave soon. We weren't even sure she had a son, but we figured the real reason to be two-fold. First, she hadn't expected Anne's mother to move in with us (which she had done shortly after our getting settled). Second, and perhaps the crowning blow was "The Washing Machine Caper."

When we moved in, we found that there were not facilities for washing clothes. The laundromat was distant and expensive. Anne had seen an ad describing a used washing machine—an "Easy" (a popular brand at that time). It was said to be "Efficient and quiet with modern ringers." The owner was even willing to deliver it and the price was incredibly low. We were so thrilled that we bought it immediately. Only then did the location problem hit us. Where could we put it? Where would we get the electricity, the water and the drain? Our bathroom provided the solution. We timed the delivery of the machine to Mrs. Schaeffer's absence one day. The awareness of her scrimping ways and stern disapproval provided ample adrenaline for me to actually carry the bulky and cumbersome machine up the steps and into our spacious bathroom. (It has been said that, given strong enough motivation and incentive, a ninety-pound weakling can lift hundreds of pounds. Very true!) I quickly attached the hoses and ran a drain line into the bathtub. Luckily, there was an electric outlet to provide power. The next problem was to keep our secret from Mrs. Schaeffer. We decided that Anne and Eleanor would do the laundry only when they were certain that the landlady was out of the house. Eleanor would stand guard and watch the driveway while Anne hurriedly ran the "Easy." We felt rather sheepish about our minor chicanery, but conserved water and electricity as much as possible. It was not a comfortable situation, so we weren't terribly disappointed we were asked to leave. She did agree to let us stay until my job ended.

On our final day as we were removing the last items, Mrs. Schaeffer opened her door and, with a tone of vexation, said, "Don't forget your washing machine," and closed the door. I don't know when or how she discovered it, but when she did, she apparently decided that we were unworthy tenants.

In retrospect, the whole affair seems to have been Providential. My lay-off from Sears forced me to do some serious soul-searching and job-hunting. It paid off—big time. I was about to enter a whole new world—the one I had hoped for when I was "hitting the books" at Colorado College.

THE FOUR SEASONS

Antonio Vivaldi was a famous Italian composer, but he must have spent at least one full year in our beautiful Midwest. Brown County—a sprawling rural area in southern Indiana—could well have been the source of inspiration for his masterful composition, "The Four Seasons." Or he could have chosen any one of many places in Wisconsin, for that matter.

Having been born and raised in the Midwest, both Anne and I had a deep appreciation for each season (mosquitoes and humidity notwithstanding). Something was lacking, however. I felt the urge to move to the fabled North Woods. Well, I reasoned, it wouldn't have to be in the *woods*, as such, but the North held a special appeal to me. (Jack London's <u>Call of the Wild</u> may have influenced my spirit of adventure.). The timing was certainly right for a move. I had lost my job at Sears and we were being squeezed out of our apartment. Anne and Eleanor were willing partners in my plan.

Right on schedule, Opportunity's knock came loud and clear. Aware that the "Help Wanted" section of the Chicago Sun covered a vast area, I went to the city library and perused a current copy. To my everlasting joy, I found an ad that seemed tailored to my interests and education. The Madison, Wisconsin plant of Oscar Mayer & Co. was in search of a Management Trainee for the Personnel Department. Recent graduates were preferred.

Anne was delighted to hear of the possibility of my getting the job I had been wanting, but knew it would mean having to leave her "new family." Nevertheless, she urged me to apply as soon as possible. Fortunately, I had a resume, to which I attached a carefully worded cover letter. Oscar Mayer was a huge company with four thousand employees at the Madison plant alone, so I expected a delay in getting a reply—if, indeed, I heard from them at all. To my surprise, their reply was almost immediate. In the letter from the Director of Personnel, I was asked to report for interviews and testing in just a few days. Those "few days" were filled with considerable anxiety, of course. The anxiety was made especially keen in view of my devastating experience with General Telephone Company. Anne and Eleanor were very supportive and gave me all of the encouragement they could muster.

During the five-hour drive to Madison, Anne did her best to show her enthusiasm for the *major* changes that she was certain would occur. By the time we reached a motel not far from the Oscar Mayer plant, we were both convinced that I would be hired, and that we would soon call Madison "home."

As I was leaving for the interview the next morning, I couldn't resist saying, "Fret not, dear wife. I'll soon be bringing home the bacon." She groaned and said, "I'd *rather* have *money!*" As I drove off, throwing her a kiss, she clasped her hands in prayer and mouthed, "I'll pray for you."

❦

I was favorably impressed by everyone and everything I saw at the enormous packing plant. Every facet of the facility gave evidence of Oscar's penchant for going first class. Near the main entrance, for example, there was a pond, in the center of which multiple water-spouts danced with a refreshing choreography. The shimmering bubbles shot up in carefully programmed spouts as high as twenty feet. As I stared in awe, the entry guard smiled and said, "Wait 'til you see the flashing colors on it at night!" The fountain and the general atmosphere of elegance made the high cost of O.M. Products more understandable.

The screening process was clearly designed with elim-ination of mediocre applicants in mind. Not only were there multiple interviewers, but also, extensive intelligence testing and psychological evaluation by the staff psychologist.

The first interview was conducted by the Employment Manager, a man not much older than I. We both knew that he held the power to determine my fate. He could risk his reputation as an effective screener by referring me to the next echelon, or he could give me the old "DCU, WCY" (Don't call us, we'll call you) routine. Actually, we weren't far into the interview before our rapport and mutual approval became apparent.

The Employment Manager, Frank Dignan, was a charming fellow with a subtle and disarming Irish sense of humor. His wittiness and quick smile belied his scrupulous attention to duty. He had an excellent blend of firmness and compassion. His ramrod posture and short-cropped, reddish hair gave him an air of military rigidity. This image, too, was offset by nuanced warmth of personality.

As the interview drew to a close, I held my breath as I waited for Frank's decision. With a wry smile, he extended his hand, gave a *firm* handshake and said, "You're over the first hurdle, Frank, but the bar gets higher. An extensive battery of tests is next, and then the evaluation by our psychologist. If he approves, your final step will be an interview with our Personnel Director, Andy Wolff. I feel pretty sure you can make it. Hope you do. Good luck."

Frank was certainly right about the bar being raised on the next hurdle. The tests were multi-faceted and exclusionary. In my opinion, anyone who could meet all of the Oscar Mayer requirements would be an excellent candidate for the C.I.A. or the F.B.I. No stone was left unturned. The psychologist was a bouncy, whimsical maverick with an impish, likeable personality. He was not at all pedantic and his questions were more conversational than overtly probing. We, too, "hit it off" well and I was soon sitting across the desk from the top gun, Andy Wolff. Unlike my previous screener, this man impressed me as an enigma wrapped in a conundrum. Like Frank Dignan, he too was a rather good-looking redhead. He was an athletic, fortyish man with narrowed eyes and a perpetual semi-smile that masked any emotion. His movements were slow and deliberate. He was clearly in control—knew it, yet wore his power without arrogance. I could not see humility as one of his virtues, however.

The psychologist had obviously briefed the Personnel Director on my evaluation, because it seemed that he had almost made his decision before we met. After exchanging a few pleasantries, Mr. Wolff leaned back in his executive chair and briefly described the functions and responsibilities of the job I would hold, should I be hired. I would be working closely with the Employment Manager, screening job applicants. Despite Mr. Wolff's inscrutable demeanor, I caught a hint of satisfaction when I expressed my regard for

Frank's professionalism. At that, he asked me how soon I could take the physical exam. I was tempted to say, "*Now*—right now—like, yesterday!" Instead, with a controlled reply, it was, "At your convenience, sir." Without delay, he called the company physician's office and set an appointment for the next morning. As he cradled the receiver, and, broadening his half-smile, he said, "Assuming you get the doc's okay, we'd like you to start as soon as you can move up here." With unbridled enthusiasm, I popped up, grabbed his hand and found myself nearly whooping, "You won't regret it, Mr. Wolff. Thanks a *lot*!" Then I probably blushed, fearing that my eagerness might have been extreme. In truth, I think it was well received.

⚜

Anne's animated elation at the good news was such that she nearly broke my neck with her jubilant hug. "Hey! No break-a the merchandise! Oscar needs me," I chided. "This calls for a celebration," we chimed in unison. We found ourselves talking at the same time, apologizing, and then starting off again. It was like the first days of our wedded bliss, only better, because of the decreased anxiety and a hatful of dreams and plans; plans we could not have made without good ol' Oscar.

It was springtime—a perfect metaphor for our budding dreams. The snow had melted away, as had our anxious moments. We looked forward eagerly to the blossoming glow of summer, the crisp and brilliant autumn and the pristine snows of a Wisconsin winter. We loved the four seasons that so accurately typified life's cycles—each with its own special charm.

When we finally began to unwind, we realized that we could waste not time in finding an apartment large enough to include room and storage for Anne's mother and the considerable baggage she had gathered over the years. Arrangements would have to be made for the move, of course. We had a Studebaker coupe at the time; it was not known for its carrying capacity. Anne was (and *is*) a genius of logistics, so I knew that it would all "come together." But that was in the offing. It was now late at night and time to sleep—perchance to dream.

MOVIN' ON

W e awoke early the next morning, eager to start our search for an apartment. The local newspaper provided several options, most of which were second-floor flats. There was one, however, that caught our eye as being well suited to our needs. It was a spacious ground-floor apartment with two bedrooms, a dining room, a kitchen and a living room. As a bonus, the location was convenient to work, church and shopping. The rent was a bit steep, but worth it. Anne was so impressed that she said she would get a job as soon as we moved in. The only negative in the transaction was the landlady, Mrs. Fidele. Like many apartment owners, she apparently had been "burned" by former tenants. Skepticism was written all over her pinched, olive-toned face. Her scrawny body had a witch-like aura about it and her brow wore a perpetual frown.

After the cursory introduction formality, she asked us to complete a detailed application form and to read and sign an intimidating rental agreement. It would not have surprised us at all if she had asked to see our marriage license and birth certificates. Her frown eased noticeably, however, when she found that I had just become and Oscar Mayer employee. She was quite aware that O.M. didn't hire transients.

Still chafing from the rather unpleasant experience with our last landlady, we immediately explained that Anne's mother would be living with us and asked about laundry facilities. Fortunately, she had a washing machine that we could use—at an additional cost—and we could use her clothesline when it didn't conflict with her schedule. When she saw my fleeting frown at the "additional cost," she offered to waive it if I would shovel coal into the monstrous furnace in the basement during the winter. I readily agreed, but hoped she wouldn't ask me to crank a cooling fan for her during the summer.

As we closed the deal, there was an air of relief all around. We were thrilled to get the perfect-for-us apartment so quickly, and, despite her implacable demeanor, the sharpness of Mrs. Fidele's skepticism seemed to have been somewhat blunted.

Next on our agenda was the move from Lafayette, Indiana, to Madison, Wisconsin—another adventure in the making.

As expected, Eleanor was pleased at my having been hired and quite willing to move "wherever and whenever." I can't say that she excited or enthused about the move, because she was clearly not given to exuberance, whatever the occasion. In her own way, however, we could tell that she was happy for us. The frustrating and burdensome task of moving took a bit of the glow off our elation, however. O.M. hadn't offered to pay our moving expenses and we clearly understood. After all, I had no prior personnel experience to justify such an expense. Consequently, we decided to make inquiries to find the least expensive moving company. After considerable research, we found one that was in our budget range. Logic dictated that the less they had to take, the less the cost. Would that we had a large and roomy station wagon—but no, brother Joe had sold us a Studebaker Coupe. He did, however, let us borrow a "top carrier" so that we could stack as much as possible on the car's roof—and did we ever! After filling every inch of the trunk and half the rear seat, we piled the top carrier high with everything we could tie down. For some reason, the picture that's most clear in my mind's eye is that of mops and broom handles. We looked like the northern version of "Okies" leaving the dust bowl—but we both had dreams of better days at the end of our journey.

When we said our tearful goodbyes to the family, the sadness was somewhat softened by various joshing comments about our having converted our coupe into a small moving van. Toots said, "Hope you can handle all that weight." That was a concern that turned out to be fully justified.

As we approached the Wisconsin border, we heard—and felt—a "thumpa-thumpa." One of the tires just couldn't take the pressure any longer. To make matters worse, a snowfall—which we had initially relished—now made driving hazardous. Drifts were building up along the roadsides, making it almost impossible to ease the car off the road. And, as luck would have it, the flat tire was on the *right* rear wheel. Murphy's Law of the Highway was alive and well. On the plus side, traffic was light and I was able to maneuver the car into a farmer's driveway. The spare tire and jack were, of course, buried deep down, under the *huge* pile of clothing, carefully-packed china, etc. All of which had to be removed while battling the increasing onslaught of huge snowflakes.

My service-station experience paid off. Changing tires had, after all, been one of my many jobs as a boy. The tire change was simple enough—it was repacking the trunk that was the problem. I scratched my head, asking, "How in the world did we ever get all of this stuff in here in the first place?!" Annie, the logistics expert, showed me. "This goes here. This goes in that corner," and so on. Before long, we were brushing the snow off each other and scurrying back into the car. As we closed the doors, Eleanor—speaking from her rear-seat blanket cocoon—merely said, "I knew you could do it, Boy," (she often called me "Boy").

As we slowly backed out and pulled away, I tried to soften the air of anxiety by saying, "The other tires look good—and they certainly won't get over-heated in this snow." That comment drew a strained, "Uh-huh," from Anne and Eleanor. Happily, the windshield wipers worked and we managed to ease our way down the highway to Madison without incident.

When we finally slid to a stop in front of our apartment house, we breathed a collective sigh of relief. With a blend of anxiety and anticipation, Anne said, "Well, Mom, there it is!" Eleanor replied, "Did you see that curtain move? Someone's watching us." "That's probably our landlady, Mrs. Fidele. She's short on charm, but long on skepticism. You have to learn how to deal with her, but it'll be okay." And, indeed, it was. The introductions went smoothly and I even caught a hint of a flickering smile when she met Eleanor. The age similarities probably helped and I supposed Mrs. F. figured El would keep us "young folk" from getting too rowdy. The fact that I would soon be shoveling coal to heat the huge building didn't hurt either.

Although we had to climb five or six steps to reach our ground-floor apartment, we soon had everything out of the car and into the house. Our enthusiasm made light work of it. The exhilaration we felt was intensified ten-fold when we saw the moving van pull up that afternoon. By nightfall, the beds were assembled and we cheerfully collapsed into them. There had been no objection to my suggestion that we have Oscar Mayer bacon the next morning... My loyalty had already begun.

PRETTY BABY

───※───

Writing about work in a meat packing/process-ing plant is not a task I would choose. Nor do I intend to upset the reader with gory details.

Although my training included exposure to all facets of meat preparation, cutting, processing, et cetera, most of my work was administrative and, eventually, managerial—thank Heaven. Work "on the floor" in a meat processing plant is not for the faint of heart. I quickly learned that I was more in tune with the vegetarians—at least I had a more tolerant attitude toward that group of people. There is something to be said for both ends of the spectrum, and *much* to be said for the middle ground. It wasn't very long, however, before I adapted to my new environment and adjusted to the seamy side of meat processing. Despite witnessing the preparation and "manufacturing" of sausage, wieners, bologna, et al, I soon became inured to it all and resumed "normal" eating habits. In fact, to this day I enjoy Oscar Mayer meat products.

My initial assignment as a Management Trainee was in the Employment section—screening, testing, and evaluating prospective employees. This evolved into increasingly responsible positions: Safety Director, Medical Department Manager, and finally, Training Director. All of the supervisors and foremen were older than I; some were twice my age. Nevertheless, we had excellent rapport and the primal knots in my stomach were soon untied. The work was challenging, stimulating and rewarding. There were, of course, many potholes in my road to the future.

<hr/>

While working in an insurance office in Madison, Anne began to experience inexplicable lower abdominal pain. She tried to endure it, but wisely decided to see a physician. He promptly referred her to a gynecologist who recommended immediate surgery. As a result, she was rendered unable to bear a child. As an "only child," she had long dreamed of having a large family of her own. The pain of the loss has long remained, but softened by the option open to us: adoption. We applied as soon as Anne was able.

Making application to adopt a child was an experience fraught with an unfamiliar admixture of emotions—and many "what-ifs." The administrator at the Catholic Welfare Agency had seen the likes of us many times, so he did have a rather clear sense of our anxiety. He assured us that they would use great care in their search for a baby whose parents would have ancestry similar to ours. We had explained that the baby's gender was of no great concern to us and hoped that this factor would expedite the process. "Expedite" was apparently a foreign word to the agency. *Two years* were to pass before a child was finally offered to us. During that period, we were tested, interviewed, scrutinized and subjected to unannounced "visits." One would think we were applying for a top-secret job in the Pentagon—but we didn't mind, so long as the end result was favorable—and it was.

In late May of 1954, we (Eleanor included) took a train to Niagara Falls, New York for a brief holiday. When we informed the adoption office that we would be away over the long Memorial Day weekend, the lady seemed a bit anxious when she said, "Be sure to call us when you get back—and, oh—have fun." We did. The falls were full and the spring weather was invigorating. I wanted to take Anne to see my old Air Force alma mater, Syracuse University, while in New York State, but we had very limited time and even more limited funds.

The "long weekend" was all too short, but it was a stimulating change of pace. Several times during the trip we found ourselves pondering over the reaction of the adoption agency lady when we told her we'd be away for a few days. At one point, Anne even said, "You don't think that she—that they—I mean, surely, if they *knew* anything—If they finally found..." I interrupted, "Now, Anne, I'm not being negative, but I think we should lower our expectations. If nothing happens—well, we've been "toughing it out" for two years; we can hang on a little longer if we have to." But *my* frustration was growing steadily, too. What was taking so long? Were they dragging their feet, or were adoptable children that hard to find? Whatever their reasons for the seemingly interminable delay, they were beyond our control. Que sera, sera.

A few of the fellows in the office knew about my mother-in-law going to Niagara Falls with Anne and me, so I was subjected to some good natured needling when I returned to work.

Shortly after lunch on my first day back, I received a phone call from Anne. Her normally alto voice came in as high soprano as she squealed, "It's here! She's here! The agency just called and said they have a little girl for us! We can pick her up at the foster-parents' home *now*! Today! How soon can you get here?" I wanted to ask questions, but didn't dare waste a second. "As soon as I tell my boss, I'm *out* of here! I'll see you in a few minutes." Andy smiled broadly at the news, hit me on the shoulder and said, "Congratulations, "Dad"—now get out of here."

As I rushed toward home I suddenly realized that I was *way* over the speed limit. I was so eager to get home, however, that I decided to risk a citation. Surely the officer wouldn't cite me if I said, "We're having a baby!" Luckily, it didn't happen and I made it to the apartment in record time.

Anne is characteristically cheerful and bubbly, but those adjectives were hardly adequate to describe the elation—the sheer joy that shone in her sparkling eyes. Even Eleanor had a broad smile as she hugged us and said, "Better get a move on, Boy." It was one of the very few times that she did not accompany us. She showed good judgment and respect for the drama of the moment that was to change our lives forever.

The forty mile trip to the foster home took us about thirty-five minutes, as I recall. Upon our arrival, we were greeted by Mrs. Drew, a smiling, plump woman who we guessed to be in her late fifties. Having some concept of our impatience, she ushered us toward the bedroom. As we scurried down the hall, we could hear the child crying. "I think she knows something big is happening," the lady said. "Have you chosen a name for her?" "Jane," we replied—perhaps a little too loudly to give reality to the heady moment. Anne added, "We've had two years to think about it and decided on "Jane," the name of my aunt, if we got a girl, and "Timothy," Frank's confirmation name, if it was a boy. We figured it would be wise to pick a short name to go with our long last name. "Tim" or "Jane" were both just right. Jane's middle name will be Eleanor, for my mom."

Then, there she was, face screwed up and wailing as if to say, "Get me out of this crib!" "A real set of lungs, she has," Mrs. Drew declared. "Oh, but she's *beautiful*!" Anne beamed. Then she picked Jane up as if she'd been entrusted with a priceless Ming Dynasty vase. As the crying ebbed and the face showed more composure, we saw a cute, chubby little girl with a pug nose, reddish hair and cerulean blue eyes. We bundled her up, gave our "thank you" to Mrs. Drew and were soon on our way back to Madison.

Anne snuggled next to me, holding Jane in her left arm (no seat belts or bucket seats at the time). We had scarcely left the driveway when Jane grabbed my right index finger and held it tightly as she fell into a deep sleep. Making my first happy sacrifice as a new father, I held my arm motionless all through the forty-mile return trip. She never let go until we reached the apartment. There was a terrible ache in my right arm, but that was overshadowed by the joy in my heart. The years of waiting were over. We had our little girl.

As if on cue, Jane awakened as I stopped the car at the apartment. Eleanor rushed out the front door, almost laughing with excitement, saying, "Let me see her! Let me hold her!" Anne's mother usually had a rather staid, almost stoic demeanor, but at this happy event, she was radiant with smiles of pure delight. A proud grandmother at last.

In the glow of this cheerful atmosphere, I turned to Anne and with a wry grin murmured, "I'll bet even Mrs. Fidele will smile when she sees Jane." Sure enough, it wasn't long before she found an excuse to come to our door. Feigning surprise at seeing her new little renter, she not only smiled, but added, "A beautiful child—a real beauty." It was a time like no other—for each of us.

At work the next morning, in answer to a barrage of questions, I proudly affirmed that I was now the father of a cute little "blue-haired, red-eyed" baby girl. Amid peals of laughter, Frank Dignan, affecting a serious tone, asked, "Gee, Frank, are you saying that you went to Niagara Falls over the holiday, and had a baby the day you got back? Hmmm..." "Now cut that out!" I roared—and the office staff justifiably continued to take advantage of my high state of excitement. They shared our joy and playful kidding proved it to me. But, *many* times thereafter, as I would pass someone in the hall, for example, he would ask, "Hey, Frank, how's that little red-eyed, blue-haired girl doing?" When I told Anne, she couldn't contain her laughter as she exclaimed, "You *didn't!*" "Oh, but I did," said I—and we've often laughed about it since.

We arranged for Jane to be baptized and assumed that that would complete our efforts in the adoption process. Not so. There were myriad forms to complete and documents to have certified. Eventually we appeared with Jane before a judge who was to bring closure to the long ordeal. Frowning, he carefully reviewed the many documents. Anne squeezed my hand and closed her eyes in silent prayer. (The judge had the power to approve or deny the adoption). Closing the dossier he raised his eyes somberly over pince-nez glasses and rumbled in a dreary voice, "Bring the child forward." I steadied Anne as she carried the small bundle toward the bench. Our awareness of Jane's occasional unprovoked outbursts heightened our tension. But, to our utter delight and total surprise, just as the judge leaned over to determine that it was, indeed, the child described in the documents, Jane opened her eyes and gave an angelic smile! The previously stoic judge smiled, too. He softly uttered the words we had so often heard before, "A beautiful child—a *real* beauty." Then, still smiling, he looked at us and pronounced, "You are now officially the adoptive parents of Jane Eleanor Balensiefer." Anne sniffled and the tears began to flow. I don't think there was a dry eye in the chamber—well, perhaps the judge was an exception, but his unexpected smile had said it all.

As we walked down the courthouse halls, trying to absorb the impact of the momentous event, an elderly couple approached us from the opposite direction. When they glanced at Jane's exposed face, the lady— smiling brightly—exclaimed, "Oh, what a *pretty* baby!" "And she's *mine*! She's *ours*!" Anne nearly shouted. Then she blushed as the couple gave me a look that said, "So? We didn't *think* it was someone *else's*." After they had passed, I said, "We're going to have to get used to this." We did—but we never tired of the words—"What a pretty baby!"

CLIMB EVERY MOUNTAIN

Climbing the corporate ladder required perseverance, strength in many areas, a dose of luck, and
a favorable impression on superiors; the latter was one
of the most difficult. A broad range of personalities
made it nearly impossible to appeal to all. By the grace
of God, I somehow managed to get favorable reviews
from enough management personnel to put me on the
next rung, and the next and so on.

But there was more to the climb than one's own
achievements in all areas; approval of one's *wife* was
quite important component. In my case, that didn't
even present a low hurdle. Everyone who ever met
Anne immediately loved and admired her. Convincing *her* of this was no easy task, however. In what (I
later presumed) was a subtle ingredient in the wife-
evaluation process, Anne and I were invited to have
dinner at the home of the Plant Training Director,
Quentin Young. This was especially intimidating for

both of us, because he was the man whose decision could make or break my promotion.

Questions plagued us—How should we dress? Were the Youngs formal? Informal? Casual? (We were painfully aware of the critical importance of first impressions). As we nervously fingered our wardrobes, we concluded that the conservative approach would be best—nothing avant-garde or au courant. That matter settled, I wondered aloud, "What if they offer us a drink? If we refuse, will they think we're too puritanical? If we accept, will we be failing their own brand of sobriety test?" We decided to merely hope that they would be like most hosts and offer us a variety of choices. Soft drinks would probably be an option we could choose. (Neither of us drank *any*thing alcoholic at that time.) We remembered the old maxims, "To thine ownself be true," and "Let the chips fall where they may."

Anne had gone to a hairstylist and every hair was neatly in place as she stepped into the bathtub. Aware of how nervous she was, I said, "Hey! You look great! I hope Mrs. Young won't be jealous." "You like my new hairdo then?" "Love it," I beamed.

She smiled in appreciation as I turned to leave the room. I hadn't taken two steps when I heard her give a bloodcurdling scream. "No! Oh, *no*!! Dear God, what will I do!?" "Anne! What happened?" (I thought she had severely cut herself.) "My *hair*! I went to fill the tub and the *showerhead* was on! My hair is *soaked*!

I can't go looking like <u>this</u>—and we have less than an hour. Oh, Frank..." Then she started to cry. Her face was red; her eyes were red; her hair was like a dripping wet-mop. I didn't mind my bathrobe getting soaked as I tried to comfort her with a compassionate hug. Fortunately, I did *not* use our standard "chin up" acronyms, "WPT" (We'll Pull Through) or "EGBOK" (Everything's Gonna Be O.K.) They would have sounded *extremely* hollow at that point. Softly, I said, "We'll think of something." "Like *what*?!" she shouted. I had no answer. As our minds raced for a solution, Anne's eyes widened with excitement. She screamed, "A *hat*! I have a nice hat! I'll dry my hair as much as possible. I can cover most of it with a hat." (Hats were worn most places during that era.) "I'll turn the oven on, towel-dry my hair while it's heating, then turn it off and stick my head in." "Whoa! Are you sure that's safe?" I was worried. "You must not have been here when I've done it before. I'll be careful. I'm *more* worried about how *long* it will take." Her hair wasn't quite dry when time finally ran out. We *had* to leave. With surprising aplomb, she adjusted the hat for maximum coverage. With more anxiety-driven sighs, we were off to the Youngs. Before Anne could enter the car, I cupped her chin in my hands, smiled approvingly and said, "You look *terrific*! I am *so* proud of you." With misty eyes, she said, "You'll ruin my mascara."

Quite often, we find that our worst fears are not realized. We hoped that such would be the case as I lifted the Young's heavy brass doorknocker. It slipped from my moist fingers and came down with a resounding "clack." Our heightened emotions amplified the sound ten-fold. The large colonial door opened promptly and Mr. and Mrs. Young greeted us warmly. So gracious and hospitable were they, that our anxious moments were soon all but forgotten. Although they did have cocktails, they made us feel quite comfortable with our having chosen soft drinks. Nor was conversation a problem.

At one point Pamela Young casually asked, "Oh, Anne, may I take your hat?" At that, Anne gave me a quick, furtive glance. Counting heavily on the Young's good nature, I grinned broadly and said, "Go ahead, Anne. Tell them about the hat." She was trapped, of course, and couldn't dare react with petulance. With flushed face and briefly downcast eyes, she gave an embarrassed, "Wellll..." and proceeded to tell them what had happened. They laughed, but showed genuine compassion. Mrs. Young took Anne by her arm and said, "Come on, Anne, let's see what we can do with that hair—and no more Mr. and Mrs. Young. It's Pamela and Quentin." Anne beamed with appreciation for the genial way her problem was handled. Instead of the hair problem causing a disastrous evening, it turned out to be the best of icebreakers. All pretense at prim ceremony melted away quickly. Any slight doubt about Anne's being "approved" was promptly and clearly dispelled. They *loved* her.

After the superb dinner, Anne helped Pamela clear the table and serve dessert. We then gave our "thank yous" and "goodbyes" and drove off under a bright moon, relieved and happy. Smiling wryly, I said, "That 'hat trick' really worked in our favor tonight, but I do think I'd better fix that showerhead." "I'm not taking any chances. I'll wear a shower cap next time…If only we could have a *home* hair dryer. They make them, you know." I gave a non-committal, "Uh huh."

⸺⸺⸺

I'll never know the exact impact "the night of the hat" had on my career. I only know that thereafter, Quentin championed my cause and I soon was awarded the promotion I had hoped for. I was initially given responsibility for the Medical, Safety, and Insurance departments, each a burden unto itself. The top of the ladder was coming more clearly into focus.

It wasn't long before I was called into Andy Wolf's inner sanctum where, to my surprise, Quentin Young sat, wearing a Cheshire cat smile. With little fanfare, Andy said, "Quentin's moving up to *Corporate* Training Director." As I congratulated Quentin, Andy said, "That creates a vacancy here. Quent recommends *you*, Frank. Think you can handle it?" Dazed, I almost blurted out, "You gotta be kidding!" but checked my impulse in time and answered, "I'm *sure* I can." "Good. You'll work as Quent's understudy for a while before we cut the cord." The simile struck me as a little frightening—but somehow appropriate. I would be taking on a new life. In effect, I was to become a teacher: an instructor. I would have to develop my own curricula, visual aids and techniques. And facing a group of skeptical and seasoned supervisory personnel was to be a formidable task. This became painfully clear when Quentin introduced me to the somber group of about thirty men. There was a distinct silence, but their thoughts rang out loudly in my supersensitive mind. "Why, he's just a *kid*!" "Probably a bookworm." "Nobody can fill Quentin's shoes." Getting their approval seemed like an impossible dream. I tried to conceal my dejection.

Having received no welcome from the men, I left the meeting feeling quite depressed. Aware of this, Quent put his hand on my shoulder. "They're a good solid group, Frank, but it took several meetings before I was able to gradually win them over. I have faith in you. Just give it some time." His encouragement notwithstanding, my melancholy was readily apparent to Anne the minute I walked into the apartment that evening. She shared my vexation and concern when I detailed the day's experience. "But this is what you've been working for! Don't worry; they'll warm up to you in no time. I believe in you—and so does Quent. It'll be okay." She hugged me warmly and, for the moment, I did feel better. I tried to convince myself that I was merely being too sensitive—that maybe it was just "stage fright." Sleep did not come easily that night, but I began the next day with determination to conquer my feeling of insecurity. I adopted a resolute and valiant façade of self-confidence. Then, under Quentin's masterful tutelage, I began to really believe in my ability to gain the group's approval. By *pretending* to be bold and brave, I eventually took on those traits.

After a number of shared training sessions Quentin came into my office one day and announced that he was leaving for the corporate office in Chicago the next week. I knew that this was inevitable, but the occasion was comparable to my first solo flight as an Air Cadet. It was a mixed bag of excitement and fear. "You don't need me anymore anyway. You're ready to fly on your own." I smiled at the metaphor. "You've been a great mentor, Quent. I won't let you down." And I didn't. My solo "flight" was a smooth one and the chill I had felt at the first meeting soon became just a bad memory. It had taken time and effort, but the fellows eventually made it clear that I was accepted as their new Training Director. One supervisor's casual comment did more to lift my spirits than he could ever imagine. He cheerfully said, "Y'know, Frank, I really look forward to these training sessions, and I'm not alone." All of the agonizing, the planning, the preparation, the "sweat and tears," were rewarded beyond measure by that one simple sentence. The feeling I had been hoping and praying for finally came—I was no longer thought of as "just a greenhorn college kid."

THIS OLD HOUSE

A partment living was satisfactory, but the rent payments yielded no equity whatsoever. Common sense told us that it would be wise to be putting that same money into the purchase of a house. We spoke to a realtor and found an affordable place within days. "Affordable" required compromises, of course. Location, condition of the house, age and amenities had to be negotiable in order to get the price we needed. As a consequence, we bought a small older house in a very modest neighborhood.

It was a mild fall day when we signed the papers. Little did we know what winter would bring.

The house had two bedrooms, a kitchen, a living room and a basement. It had a large front yard with a white fence and the general image of a rather attractive, quaint cottage. The garage was a separate, offset building. In our eagerness and naiveté, we failed to notice that the "driveway" (two strips of concrete) to the garage sloped downward. This presented no problem during the halcyon days of autumn, but then came the freezing rain and snow. Because of the wrong-way slope and a severe freeze, the garage door was soon tightly sealed by a ten-inch barrier of solid ice. My axe-wielding efforts were ineffectual. There was an up side to the problem, however. The tiny garage was still too packed with unopened moving boxes to provide room for the car ... The thought of it being entombed in an icy sepulcher chilled me. There *was*, however, a small side door toward the rear of the garage through which we could gain access to our boxes.

With the devastating onslaught of winter, we discovered that ice was not confined to the outside of the house. Jack Frost placed intricate and artistic patterns on our bedroom windows and the sills became repositories for ice cakes. As the room warmed, they became water puddles.

Heat was provided by a small basement furnace with one vent in the center of the living room floor. It was exceptionally inefficient, but we survived the winter. After all, we were young, healthy and happy to be in our own home, despite the flaws. Of course, we eagerly looked forward to signs of springtime. But the thaw at winter's end was to add a thorny new chapter to our learning experience.

In late April, a gradual warming trend was a mixed blessing. Higher temperatures meant melting ice.

Melting ice meant water run-off. In our case, the run-off became the "run-*in*." The basement—with its washing machine, storage boxes, et cetera—was soon flooded. In a desperate effort to solve the problem, I discovered that the previous owners had installed an electric sump-pump. Elated, I snaked the drain hose through a window, flicked the switch on and welcomed the hum and the sucking sound. I ran up the stairs to shout the good news to Anne and Eleanor. Jane clapped her hands as she shared in the moment's excitement. And only a "moment" it was. As our joyful sounds diminished, so did the sound of the sump-pump. We heard a slow "chugga-chugga," then an awful silence. Our two year old Jane began to cry as she saw our pained expressions and heard us groan, "Oh, *no!*" The only solution—a temporary one—was a bucket brigade. After the exhausting experience I dashed to the hardware store, bought a new pump and installed it before nightfall. Drained of energy, we collapsed into bed. We awoke the next morning with newfound vigor and enthusiasm. The new pump had done its job and we began to feel more secure. This feeling, too, was short-lived. As I was finishing breakfast, Anne spoke with obvious reluctance. "Frank, I hate to tell you this, but we have a roof leak. I just saw water drip from the living room ceiling." Deflated, I grabbed a ladder and climbed to the attic through the small ceiling entry port in the hall. Having quickly found the source of the leak, I called to Anne for something to catch the drip. Eleanor replied that she would donate a very old and very thick winter coat. This I promptly spread over the wet area then placed a bucket on it. Fortunately, the leak was in only one location, so the bucket was adequate during the rainstorm. I was able to repair the roof the next day, but felt that the water problems might just be the tip of the iceberg—so to speak. We also eventually concluded that the house was either ghost-ridden or poorly plumbed. Doors would open or close of their own volition. Located on a winding street, we called it "The Little Crooked House on the Little Crooked Street." Quite dispirited, we were unaware of the *much* brighter days that lay ahead.

One happy occurrence during our brief tenure deserved to be told.

Some friends of ours had informed us that an attractive young single schoolteacher friend was coming from Wisconsin to spend the weekend with them. My college chum, Bob Finucane, was also still single, so we asked him down to meet Nancy Dupuis. Never having met her, we could only hope that she would be appealing and engaging enough to keep Bob awake. (He had fallen asleep on several of the blind dates we had previously arranged.)

We had long hoped that Bob would find "the right girl," marry her and settle down. Knowing Bob's insouciance toward most women, we decided to set the stage for a romantic evening and just hope that the right chemistry and spark would ignite a lasting love affair.

Our friends, the Huths, dropped Nancy off at an appointed time on Saturday evening. The teacher stereotype she definitely was not! The Huths' adjective, "attractive," was highly inadequate. Her raven hair, large dark eyes, sensuous lips and petite, seductive figure would turn any man's head. I found myself thinking, "This *has* to be 'Miss Right.' Stay awake this time, Bob, for Heaven's sake!" One look at Nancy and the sometimes phlegmatic Robert suddenly came to life. He was clearly favorably impressed—as well he should have been. Her infectious laugh and wholesome, yet sexy demeanor inspired Bob's—and our—rapt attention.

After a lovely candlelit dinner, Anne showed her usual prescience by serving *strong* coffee with dessert—"just in case." With pre-arranged guile, I selected the most romantic phonograph record available. It was Jackie Gleason's "Music for Lovers Only." One would have to be comatose to be unmoved to strong feelings of amour. On cue, Anne cheerily asked if I would clear the table of the dishes while she went to check on Jane. I agreed but said, "First, let's have some music." As I started the record, I said to Nancy, "Bob may have two left feet, but I'll bet you could teach him how to dance." "I'll try," was her cautious reply.

We stretched our out of the room time as long as we could. When we peeked in, we were delighted to see them dancing cheek-to-cheek. Bob had taken the bait and was hopelessly hooked.

Whatever part the music, the dinner, or Nancy's obvious charm played—the end result couldn't have been better. They married several months later and eventually had an enviably beautiful family—one girl and three boys. Bob finally lost his reputation for dozing off while on a date.

Tragically, Nancy was to lose her life to cancer while the children were still quite young. Bob's father also died, and his mother moved in and became a marvelous stabilizing force as an exemplary surrogate mother. The moniker Bob gave to his mother, Florence, was "Florrie, the Tough Old Swede." Tough but gentle, she lived a full, active life and died at one hundred four!

A COTTAGE FOR SALE

A fter enduring considerable frustration and irritation with maintenance and repair, we decided to sell "The Crooked Little House" and have a new one built. Grateful and happy to live with us, Anne's mother offered to help us financially. We promptly made arrangements with a contractor and staked a "FOR SALE" sign in our front yard. We hoped to avoid realtor fees by selling the place ourselves. An ad in the local paper brought several people to our door, most of whom were polite in their rejection.

As construction on our new home progressed, our worry increased. What if we couldn't sell the old house?! I made every physical improvement I could and Anne put her interior decorating skills to work. We could then only wait and pray for a buyer.

A couple who had shown only mild interest in our house returned with their two year old grandson several days after their initial visit. As we reiterated every positive note we could think of, Jane gave the little boy a tour of the place, acting as a two-year-old saleslady. As we spoke to our prospective buyers, their grandson and Jane came running into the room. "I *wuv* this house, Grandpa. *Pwease* buy it! Pwease?" We all chuckled and when Jane said, "You can have Gramma's old coat, too!" we all laughed in earnest. Anne calmly joked, "That's right, honey, and I'll throw in my old sweater. Now show Jimmy the new game we bought you." My flushed face went unnoticed as I recalled having left Eleanor's old, rain-soaked coat in the attic. Jane apparently remembered all too well. But she did a great job of convincing Jimmy—who, in turn, influenced his doting grandparents. They bought the house!

After the deal was finally closed, we raised a toast to Jane, our two-year-old real estate agent. We quickly changed the subject when she blurted out, "I hope they like your coat, Gramma."

<hr>

Wisconsin had it all—ice and snow in winter; rain and slush in spring; heat, humidity and cargo-carrying mosquitoes in summer; but breathtaking beauty in fall. Nut trees; cheese factories; breweries; rolling, dairy-dotted hills. Good and bad—we loved it, and could hardly wait to move into our new house on Eyre Lane. (It was pronounced "Eerie," but that didn't scare us. After all, we had been dealing with door-closing ghosts for some time.)

A descriptive title for the home-building experience would be, "The Agony and the Ecstasy"—with emphasis on "The Agony"—especially for inexperienced first-time builders.

Part of our agreement with the Rigbys—the buyers of our old home—required that we vacate the place within thirty days. Getting a contractor to finish building "on schedule" was a daunting task—whoever or whatever might cause delays. Unavailable supplies; equipment failure; rain; worker sicknesses; Murphy's Law; incorrect paint color—we dealt with it all—and our "30-day Novena" got results. On the 29th day, we moved out of the Little Crooked House and into our charming, ghost-free colonial house with white trim. With French windows, oak cabinets and a raised-hearth fireplace, we felt that we had bought a little bit of Heaven.

There was a small pond near our property that was excellent for ice-skating in the winter. Of course, it was also an open invitation to the "cargo-carrying" mosquitoes to which I referred earlier.

Our neighbors were in our age group and had similar tastes and interests. They also had children about Jane's age. We became such good friends with the "Erye Lane gang" that there are some with whom we still communicate.

Most of our memories of life on Eyre Lane are pleasant ones; there is one notable exception. One day I received a call at work from Anne. In a distraught and anxious voice she pleaded, "Please come home right away! Our basement is flooded. Boxes are floating!" "But the contractor *assured* me ... never mind. I'll be right there." I rushed into by boss' office sputtering, "Our basement's flooded. Anne needs me." "Didn't you have that same problem with your other house?" he asked. "It's a recurring nightmare," was all I could say.

On the way home I stopped to buy *another* sump-pump—something I never dreamed I would have to do again. An unwelcome and vexing déjà vu.

The damage to the boxes and to the various loose items was not severe, but the stress and physical effort were significant. My strong words of complaint to the contractor paid off. He promptly constructed a concrete barrier around each window-well—the places that had let the rainwater flow in. We had no similar problems thereafter. I knew then that we could sell *that* house with a clean conscience, should we ever have to. Little did I realize that, in a few short years, we would be doing just that.

NEW WORLD SYMPHONY

While stationed at the Santa Ana, California air base, I recalled only the better features of Midwest living. I believe I missed the distinct four seasons most of all. The freshness and beauty of spring rebirth; the gigantic and plentiful shade-trees swaying in a summer shower; the crisp brilliance of fall color and the pungent aroma of a burning leaf pile; the thrill of the first snowfall, generating dreams of a white Christmas. But, as a lonely cadet, I happily ignored the down side of it all. Time and distance had blurred my vision of reality.

After several years of Wisconsin's extremely cold winters, and hot, humid, mosquito-plagued summers, the benefits of Southern California living became increasingly appealing.

Aware of an Oscar Mayer branch plant in Los Angeles, my thoughts began to stray westward. What if an opening developed in the West Coast personnel office? What if my qualifications were a perfect match? What if I were awarded the dream transfer—including moving expenses? The ocean; the mountains; the vineyards and citrus groves comprised a vision of Paradise. The thought that a meatpacking plant could be part of Paradise amused me, but I felt that such could be the case.

My route to and from work took me past St. Mary's—a lovely old red brick church. As my wish for a transfer to California became more fervent, I began to make regular stops at the church to pray for a miracle. I felt it would take a miracle to get all the stars aligned in my favor.

The days dragged on and hope began to fade. I knew that the Los Angeles branch was much smaller that the Madison plant and that there was little turnover. My only hope was that the L.A. plant would grow and create more openings. As I was thinking, "Fat chance of that happening," I learned that the L.A. plant personnel manager was going to visit our Madison facility. Could this be the start of something big, or just a source of disappointment and envy? Whatever the significance of his visit, I was eager to meet Bill Koch, and to learn more about the West Coast operation. I decided to lower my expectations and to stifle my illusions.

On Mr. Koch's first day at our plant, I was designated his "tour guide." I found him to be a rather low-key, likeable man in his mid-forties. We got along quite well and he soon asked me call him "Bill." Although he was obviously interested in the differences in our operation and his, he was more conversational than I had expected. He showed considerable interest in my family and in me—my duties, responsibilities, my capabilities and interests. He even asked me to join him for a drink after work. I felt flattered but uneasy because of my lack of "drinking" experience. It was something of a dilemma, in that I wanted to appear mature and comfortable in a barroom setting.

We met in the lounge of Bill's hotel. Bill had arrived shortly before I did, and I could see that he had already finished a drink. He greeted me with a broad smile, a hearty handshake and a "What'll you have, Frank?" A waiter was standing by as I snapped with self-assurance, "Make mine a 7 and 7." I didn't know what it was, but a friend had told me that he liked it. I assumed it meant seven parts water and seven parts of whatever. I would then be having only half a drink, as I figured it. I caught Bill's knowing grin as he ordered "another scotch-rocks, waiter." "Wow!" I thought. "Straight whiskey! —and he's already had one. Must be a heavy drinker." I was even more convinced when he showed none of the "tipsy" signs as he quaffed his third scotch.

The drinks arrived promptly. With a mutual, "Cheers," we clinked glasses and I took my first sip. "Whoa!

This stuff is *potent*" was my first reaction, but, not wanting to appear the "country bumpkin," I smiled casually and, nearly choking, squeaked, "Not bad." I took some water—hoping to dilute the impact of the cocktail—and began to "nurse it along." In very short order, Bill summoned the attentive waiter with, "Two more of the same." Feeling certain that Bill would be upset if I refused, I gave a breezy, "Why not?" while my mind raced for a solution to the dilemma. That solution presented itself in two well-timed and well-placed conditions. One was a potted plant near my elbow and the other was a timely parade of shapely females. As I would whisper, "Take a look at *that* one!" I would quickly and covertly dump most of my drink into the planter. I was rather proud of my achievement as I made it through happy hour without a hitch. I dared not think of how I would handle the next similar circumstance.

With the exception of alcohol, I found that Bill and I were compatible. We shared similar attitudes, principles and values. We were both happily married but had well-honed eyes for the svelte female form. We, of course, considered it "art appreciation."

The next morning, after a closed-door meeting of the two Personnel Managers, Andy, my boss, called me in to join them. "Bill and I have been talking and—well, you explain, Bill." My heart began to pound as my hopes reached their peak. "The L.A. plant's grown so much that I'm beginning to feel like a one-armed paper hanger. I need an assistant, and I think you'd be a perfect fit for the job, Frank. What do you say?" I had rehearsed this scene at St. Mary's for months. "To tell you the truth, this is just what I've been hoping for and working toward. No offense, Andy; you've been a grand boss—a perfect mentor. I've learned a great deal from you—so much so that I now feel well equipped to handle more responsibility. Thanks for your vote of confidence, Bill. I'd love to have the job." "What about Anne? Will she be willing to move to the coast?" I almost laughed. "Actually, this has been a dream for *both* of us. I think she's mentally packed our bags a hundred times." "Hate to lose you, Frank, but I can't blame you. Bill's a good man." Andy shook my hand firmly, and, to my utter surprise, I saw that his eyes were moist. It was a dramatic and pivotal point for each of us. "Bob in Purchasing will help you work out the moving details. Now get a move on and tell Anne to start packing—for real!"

On my way home I stopped in at St. Mary's for a heartfelt "Deo Gracias." My request had been granted and a new and exciting chapter in my life in my life was about to begin.

Anne nearly jumped for joy, shouting, "I'm so *proud* of you! I *knew* you could do it. When do we leave?" Meanwhile, Anne's mother just smiled with a "Congratulations, Boy." Jane was understandably bewildered by the sudden excitement, but soon shared the celebratory mood of the moment. We did, of course, experience some fleeting pangs of anxiety and disliked the thought of leaving our friends and neighbors. Jane was too young to have developed any close friends.

That night, unable to sleep, we found ourselves packing our best china with gusto. The moving company was to pack and deliver anything we wanted, but some items were too precious to entrust to whom Anne called "total strangers who might be careless." Anne's mother, Eleanor's, "collection" had me worried. Eleanor had been a rock collector for *years*. I don't think she ever saw a rock she didn't like. Consequently, our houses' exterior periphery looked like a rock quarry, as did our basement, although most of the rocks were in boxes. Those boxes, incidentally, stood noticeably immobile while many others floated during the flooding to which I alluded earlier.

Doubting that the interests and accoutrements of mothers-in-law were even remotely considered in moving expense calculations, I was justifiably concerned about the weight factor. I managed to collect several *strong* boxes—about 20"x20"x12"—and reluctantly began filling them with every geologic variety known. Eleanor, Anne and even Jane did the same, although much of their time was spent admiring each rock, pebble and stone. Exasperated, I muttered, sotto voce, "I'd like to dump them all." There were seemingly endless repetitions of, "Oh! Look at this one!" and, "I think this one came from…" and, "I'd never part with *this* one!"

We had hardly given a thought to our next home, but finally realized that I would have to fly out ahead of the rest to find one. I was blessed with a wonderful, hospitable cousin and her family who lived within driving distance of the L.A. plant. When I called and asked if I could visit them while looking for a convenient motel, Cousin Ceil Cahill insisted I stay with them until I could find a house to rent or buy. Anne took the news with mixed feelings. We would be separated for the first time. I would be a continent away and she, Eleanor and Jane could only wait and pray that I would find a suitable home. "Whatever you choose, I know we'll like it. I just hope we'll have neighbors like our Madison friends." She smiled gamely as I assured her I would avoid the ghetto and, jokingly, that I would thoroughly interview each potential neighbor before signing any contract.

My departure from the airport was predictably an emotional one, especially when Jane sobbed, "Will we ever see Daddy again?" I wondered that a bit myself as the gigantic plane lumbered along toward a shaky ascent. Once aloft, the flight went smoothly enough until we crossed the Sierras and headed for Los Angeles. A sudden turbulence shook the plane violently and without warning. Was this to be a fitting metaphor for times that lay ahead? The pilot's apology did little to calm our nerves and many of us would have kissed the ground upon touchdown were it not for the modern-day plane-to-terminal corridor.

My blithe and buoyant cousin Ceil waved enthusiastically as she saw me enter the terminal. We hadn't seen each other since Dan Hickey and I visited her during the war. It was a heartwarming reunion as Ceil's daughter, Jeannine, and husband, Bill, passed around the warm hugs.

My "room" was an alcove between the kitchen and the living room. The furniture, in total, consisted of a day bed and a nightstand, but a palatial ambience couldn't have pleased me more. I had love and support and, not to be lightly considered, free room and board. But I was careful not to abuse my privileges. No matter how gracious my host and hostess, it was imperative that I find a place for myself and my family. The logical next step would be to find a conscientious and trustworthy real estate agent. Neither Ceil nor Bill could sincerely recommend one. My eventual connection with a provocative female agent evolved into an odyssey out of Dashiel Hammett, though Sam Spade I was not.

My first day at the L.A. plant was "get acquainted" day, as expected, and Bill's need for an assistant became very apparent. I was given considerable latitude in hiring, running the medical department, handling the safety division, conducting training sessions and more. Bill was then free to devote more time to union negotiations and developmental and administrative functions. At the end of the day, Bill called me in, breathed a deep sigh and said, "I can't tell you how much it means to have you on board, Frank. What do you think of our crew?" "I think they'll be great to work with. It should be smooth sailing once I learn the ropes. Incidentally, that nurse is a knock-out." "Yeah— in fact, I think she should be wearing a sign that says 'Danger-Hazardous Material.' She knows her job, but she also knows *men*. Just be forewarned."

As I was about to leave I asked Bill if he could recommend a good realtor. Without hesitation he said that he had heard favorable comments about a Gloria Devlin; so salutary that he kept her phone number in his Rolodex file. I eagerly took the number and called her early the following morning. After hearing of my needs, she suggested that she pick me up Saturday morning and spend the day exploring several possibilities. Even before meeting her, the assurance in her sultry voice made me feel that she would provide the right house at the right price. Before returning the phone to its cradle, her soft "I can't wait to meet you, Frank," was like a warning shot across my bow. There was a prickly feeling on the back of my neck. Shouldn't she have said, "I can't wait to show you these houses I have listed?" First the nurse, now the real estate lady. Maybe it's just the way they are on the West Coast. Yeah, right. Probably just an overreaction to the headiness of my new life. Besides, I was very happily married. "What am I thinking?! All she said was, 'I can't wait to meet you, Frank.' Yeah, but the *way* she said it. Oh well—she probably talks like that to all of her clients."

The real estate lady pulled into the Cahill's driveway exactly at the appointed time—8:30. Bill, who worked Saturdays, had already left and Ceil and Jeannine were still in their pajamas. With visions of our California home dancing about during the night, I had gotten little sleep and arose early, eager to explore housing possibilities. With a quick, "Be back later," I left to meet Gloria Devlin. She had gotten out of the car and started toward the front porch as I closed the door behind me. She was a trim, "handsome" woman in a form-fitting business suit. I guessed her to be about ten years older than I. Her walk, her soft smile and general demeanor validated my first impression on the telephone. She was attractive, but not beautiful. Beauty, however, is clearly not an essential ingredient to sexiness. Her handshake was firm, but held just beyond the three-second limit decreed by protocol. I pulled away as I felt my face flush. "Glad to meet you, Mrs. Devlin." "Please call me Gloria. You don't mind if I call you Frank?" she purred. "And it's not *Mrs.* Devlin anymore. I'm divorced." "Oh, I'm sorry." I muttered. "Don't be," she smiled wryly. "I'm not." There she goes again. "The houses," I gulped. "Are they near where I work?" "Not really. After our phone conversation, I did some research and found several places that meet your needs, but they're not near the plant. We'll start with a place in Arcadia—but first—*relax*, Frank; you seem tense. Don't worry, I'll take good care of you." "Well, this *is* a mighty big step—but I'm in your hands. (*What* am I *saying*?!)" Patting my knee, she sighed, "That's better."

She was right about the houses. Each met our parameters. One, however, had the additional benefit of a Covina location near the home of a fellow Oscar employee. We could carpool.

When we left the Covina house, I told Gloria that I'd like to talk to Anne first, but felt certain she'd agree that it was the place for us. Anne, Eleanor, and Jane had flown to Tucson to stay with relatives until I could find the right house for us. When I called she said, "I'll trust your judgment. How soon can we move in?" "I'll have to talk to Gloria about the final details." "*Gloria!* Who's Gloria?" Why did I feel guilty when I said, "She's just that old real estate agent Bill recommended."

When the deal was closed and the papers signed, I thanked Gloria effusively as we sat in her car. "I'll miss you, Frank," she huskily whispered—putting her hand on my thigh. Before I could react or reply, she put her other hand behind my head and gave me a sensuous, lingering kiss. Fighting this unfair assault valiantly, I gulped, "I can't wait 'til Anne sees the house—I know she'll love it." But I don't think she heard me.

TOGETHER AGAIN

With the move-in date finally established, my first act was to give the good news to Anne. The next step was to arrange for shipment of our furniture from its Wisconsin storage. Anne was predictably ebullient and wanted to board the next plane out of Tucson (she, Eleanor and Jane were staying with cousin Joan and family). I could only imagine the degree of their excitement at the thought of moving into our Southern California home. Flight arrangements were promptly made and they were soon airborne.

The people who witnessed our reunion at the Los Angeles airport probably thought that we had been apart for *years*, so teary was our meeting. Jane was understandably full of questions. "Where's our house? Is it far away? Are there kids around?" Laughing at her excited questions, I said, "It's in Covina, not terribly far away, and yes, I think I saw a girl about your age somewhere across the street." She could hardly contain herself after learning *that* news.

I don't know how many times I heard Jane ask, "Are we there yet, Daddy?" before I was finally able to say. "Yes, honey, this is the place."

The casual observer would probably have ranked the house as "average" for Southern California at that time; in Anne's eyes, however, it was a palace right out of "The King and I." She squeezed my hand and spoke in a tone of wonder, "Frank, it's *lovely*! How did you *ever* find it?" Then quickly, "Oh, I remember, the real estate lady." "She was a real go-getter, all right." I gulped, then ushered them to the front door. Eleanor gave me a pat on the back, smiled broadly and drawled, "Well done, Boy, it's beautiful!" And it was beautiful—in *our* eyes—from every angle. Situated on a rather quiet, dead-end street, it was of the "ranch-house" genre—a low, pale green one-story house with heavy shake shingles. The convenient layout featured a used-brick fireplace and a den, in addition to the standard living/dining room, kitchen, et al. Outside, a banana tree, a castor bean tree, a palm tree, begonias and fuschia were strategically placed to create a tropical flavor. Topping off the Hawaiian motif was a long lanai that was bordered by a lush, flower-edged lawn and adjacent garage. The appealing structure had "let's party" written all over it—so to speak. It was not to idly gather dust.

When we realized that the ocean, the mountains and the deserts were but short drives away, our bliss was complete—or so we thought. There was yet another great benefit that we hadn't dreamed of.

To refer to our across-the-street neighbors as "a great benefit" would be to understate the case. They were a warm and gracious family of four: John and Betty Jo Burns and their two children, Laurie and Doug. I guessed Laurie to be around four years old and Doug around five.

The day after our arrival, Betty Jo came to introduce herself and her children. John was away at work. The timing was perfect. Jane's birthday was the following week and we saw an immediate and mutual connection between her and the Burns children. Anne had been concerned about celebrating Jane's' fourth birthday in a strange town, and with no friends to invite. Anne's query, "Would you like to come to Jane's birthday party?" prompted very toothy grins, with, "Yes!" from Laurie and "Boy, I'll say!" from Doug. Amid the ensuing laughter, it was apparent that Anne and Betty Jo also felt an immediate "connection" and mutual approval. It marked a small beginning to a friendship that has endured the test of time.

When John Burns returned from work that evening, he, too, came to welcome us. My first reaction was one of awe, as it was with Betty Jo. They *both* looked extraordinarily bronzed, attractive and healthy. Would we pale-faced Midwesterners fit in if *all* Californians looked like swimsuit models? Their tanned appearance became more understandable when John asked us to come for a dip in the pool. When he left, I growled, "Get out the suntan lotion, Anne; we're going to blend in yet!"

 Part of "blending in"—thanks to John's not-too-subtle chiding—required that I abandon my treasured gray felt hat. It was like losing my security blanket, but I trusted John's judgment. I had to agree that a homburg in Southern California was like a turban in a synagogue. I didn't give up easily, but John's needling just couldn't be ignored. I was embarrassed and a bit irritated at first, but soon realized that, as a friend, he was actually helping me adapt to my strange new world. I had to (reluctantly) thank John also for convincing me that pipe smoking—like the hat—was anything but de rigueur in Southern California. Frankly, I thought I looked quite dashing in my felt hat and cherry-wood pipe, but social conformity called for change and adjustments. The price I paid by yielding to John's wheedling proved to be well worth my temporary discomfort. It wasn't long before I noticed a sharp drop in the number of stares that seemed to ask, "Where's *he* from!?"

In due course, we found that our neighbors ran the societal gamut—friendly, aloof, gregarious, eccentric, mysterious, reclusive—*all* quite interesting—and all on our short, rather unimposing street. The Burns, however, were clearly our favorites. We shared many good times with them and remain friends nearly five decades after their warm welcome on that blustery February day.

FRIENDSHIP

W e *loved* Southern California, but were mature enough to realize that "Happiness is not just a *place*." Rather, the place—to most of us—is but one ingredient in a very complex recipe for peace, joy and serenity. Perhaps the most essential ingredients (again—to *most* people) are a shared love, and friends. Without these, the most beautiful and idyllic place can soon lose its lustre. We have been exceptionally fortunate in having an abundance of shared love *and* friends. Our place was lovely, but our friends were the icing on the cake.

The Burns—to whom I referred in the previous chapter—were our first California friends. More were to enter our lives and graduate from the casual acquaintance status to that of solid, tried-and-true friends. One such couple was John and Dorothy McGowan. Here again, the children of our friends-to-be played a vital role in the evolution of our associations. Church affiliation was also of considerable benefit in establishing acquaintances. Belonging to the same religious denomination also provided a common bond.

Shortly after we officially joined Sacred Heart Church in Covina, it was announced that the nearby St. Lucy's Priory was to have a "boutique," and the ladies were invited to attend. Anne was delighted at the thought of meeting other parishioners with common interests. The event was providential. She met two sisters, Dorothy McGowan and Mary Thomas. There was an immediate and mutual feeling of kinship. Similar principles, attitudes and philosophies blended to form a solid foundation for what was to become close, lifelong friendships. To make matters even better, Anne learned that Dorothy lived only three blocks away and had a daughter, Megan, who was Jane's age and a son, Tim, two years older. Patrick was to arrive later. Dorothy's sister, Mary Thomas and her husband, John, also lived nearby and had children in Jane's age-range. Jim and Kate were their oldest and Dave, Barb, Liz and Allison were to later round out that lovely family. The reader will undoubtedly have gleaned from these biographical data that we were surrounded by the Irish. Ah, shoor. Anne and I often chided them about trying to overwhelm us. Anne's mother, as you may recall, was pure Irish, so THAT stood for SOMETHING. I was the lonely "kraut." All of this encouraged much good-natured ribbing, but, in truth, we shared great respect and admiration.

Anne and I were particularly struck by the indomitable spirit shown by both families as they faced tragedy and trauma. Good humor and strength in the face of adversity were their "stock in trade." Prime examples of painful and untoward events were, in later years, Jim's tragic surfing accident that left him severely paralyzed for the rest of his life, and John Thomas' auto accident, resulting in pain which has never completely disappeared. The McGowans' trouble began much earlier, when they discovered that their son, Tim, was emotionally disturbed. His hostility was—to put it mildly—frightening. The combination of time, prayer and psychological help produced something of a miracle, however. Tim was to later enter a seminary and become an exemplary Catholic priest. He is currently serving God and man in a teaching capacity. Sadly, both Dorothy and Mary were to endure pain and suffering before their deaths. Both Johns have adapted bravely to their loss. Through good times and bad, they have shown courage, perseverance and an unflagging sense of humor.

As our children grew, we did a great deal of camping, traveling and exploring of California together. These experiences were enhanced by John McGowan's enthusiasm and amazing historical knowledge. He was—and is—the quintessential tour guide. Without his recommendations there would have been many points of interest and adventures missed.

There seems to be a great similarity between our cycle of life and that of—let's say—a fruit tree. A seed is planted. Life begins. Through nurturing, growth follows. Proper care often produces a fruitful harvest. And we know winter to be a temporary condition, with a blessed rebirth in the offing. There *is* hope.

WHAT KIND OF FOOL AM I?

Much of my work at Oscar Mayer & Co. involved recruiting, interviewing and testing job applicants. One of the main sources of applicants was privately owned employment agencies. As a natural consequence, I became acquainted with agency owner/managers. They, of course, "lobbied" for business by frequent visits, trivial gifts, compliments and other business developing techniques. I enjoyed dealing with them and as a matter of fact, became somewhat envious of their ability to earn a good income by their wits and self-governance. The owner/manager of a job-placement service was a self-employed, independent contractor. He was, as the vernacular has it, "his own boss."

Phil Crane, an agency owner with whom I worked closely and often, invited me to a dinner meeting of placement service owners. Hoping to get a better insight into their intriguing business, I gladly accepted. To my surprise, I was called to the podium and presented with and "Employer of the Month" award. I should have saved that plaque; just as many business owners frame their business' first dollar bill. That occasion reaffirmed what had been picking away at the back of my mind for some time. Phil was happy and successful in his field, so why couldn't I be the same? My years of screening job applicants and handling all facets of personnel matters made me eminently well qualified to run a job placement service. There was a great deal that I did *not* know about running a business—state laws, rules and regulations, administrative and procedural matters—but I had the self-confidence, the will and the determination to do whatever it would take to be "on my own."

The information that I had gleaned from Phil suggested that there would be very lean times for the first several months and there were no guarantees. The business could eventually succeed or it could fail miserably. The challenge was tantalizing—so much so that I firmly decided to set my plan in motion. Careful and measured steps would be required.

As I pondered my life-changing decision, some rather sharp points of anxiety began to chip away at my somewhat cavalier attitude. My boss, Bill Koch, had invested heavily in me. As my mentor and my supervisor, he had groomed me to eventually replace him as Director of All Personnel. I owed him a lot. I wondered where I would have been without his faith in me.

I began to feel like a traitor. The employment section; the safety department; the medical department—and other areas—were dependent upon my leadership. How would *they* feel? There was always an almost palpable requirement for deeply committed *loyalty* at Oscar Mayer & Co. There were so many unwritten rules and subtle cues that it seemed to nearly reach cult status. To be an Oscar Mayer employee—especially in the upper echelon—was to be a member of the chosen few—"and don't you forget it!" was implicit but clearly understood.

Even if Bill accepted my resignation without considering me a foolhardy traitor, how was I to survive financially? Not only would I lose my rather comfortable salary, but also, there would be no more perquisites—no health insurance, no bonuses; no retirement plan, no "sick pay"—no benefits of any sort.

And, of utmost importance, what would *Anne* think? That I had lost all touch with reality? That I was tilting at windmills? Would she say, "Are you out of your mind?! You're willing to give up a wonderful job that you've worked so hard for—and all for a pie-in-the-sky, harebrained idea?!" Or would she say, "If it's what you really want, I'm with you all the way. I'll be your partner, and together we'll make a go of it."

As I sat in my office, musing these ponderous options, there was a tap on my open door. Being deep in thought, I was rather startled—more so when I saw that it was Bill. When I looked up, I saw that he was leaning against the doorjamb with a casual leg crossed, hand-in-pocket demeanor. When he spoke, it was through his unique but often employed "frown/smile" that displayed an air of bemused puzzlement. "Must be pretty serious thinking. I've been standing here, almost afraid to break your reverie." "Just weighing several options for—uh—the next training session," I lied. Was my face flushed? Did he see little beads of perspiration on my brow? Did I appear disingenuous? Whatever he thought or sensed, he handled it with his customary aplomb. "Just want to go over some figures with you. No rush. Give me a buzz when you're ready." "Right! Will do!" I replied—with perhaps a bit too much gusto. As Bill left, I could feel an ebb in the strength of my resolve. Deception and guile were beyond me. Honesty and candor had been woven into the very fabric of my being my entire life. Surely, I hadn't deceived Bill. I was relieved that he hadn't asked me point-blank what was troubling me. I might have blurted out my intentions before getting Anne's approval. I did manage to gain enough self-control before meeting with Bill. Whether by chance or by design, nothing further was said about that awkward moment when my face either flushed or turned pale. My emotions had been granted a temporary reprieve, but the day of reckoning wasn't far away—unless Anne was adamantly opposed to my plan.

The four of us who carpooled from Covina to Los Angeles got to know each other's moods and, sometimes, personal problems. On the way that evening,

Ed Reese—not one to mince words—pointedly asked, "What's eating you, Frank? You're awfully quiet tonight." "No big deal," was my blasé reply. "Just a lot of mental preparations for some upcoming training sessions." I then forced myself into light-hearted conversation to cloak the growing visceral anxiety. The traffic was heavier than usual and the drive home seemed interminable. I was reminded of Jane's incessant, "Are we there yet, Daddy?"

When we *finally* reached my house, I had to restrain my impulse to bolt from the car and dash into the house. Knowing that Anne would immediately see through any attempt of mine to hide my emotions, I wasted no time in getting straight to the point "Could we talk—alone?" Anne turned to her mother and smiled, "Mom, would you mind entertaining Jane for a while?" I followed with, "Yeah, El. We have business to discuss that would only confuse Jane." Sensing that something was afoot, she blithely said, "C'mon, Jane, let's go out and play with your beach ball." The door had barely closed before Anne faced me squarely and, with a look that combined concern and compassion asked in rapid succession, "What's wrong? What happened? Is it serious?" I hadn't realized that my anxiety was *that* transparent. "Nothing's really *wrong*, and nothing's happened—*yet*. And yes, it *is* serious—but in a good way." Then, without prologue, "Honey, how would you like it if my work was right here in Covina?" Before I could explain, the bright sparkle returned to her eyes as she asked, "Do you mean Oscar's opening a plant *here*?!" "Well...no...you see, I want to start my own business." Momentarily deflated and shocked, she dropped into a chair with, "But how? With what? Where?" I stopped her litany of queries with, "I knew you'd have a jillion questions, so please just hear me out." As she pursed her lips to restrain her urge to grill me, I laid out the series of events that led up to my reaching the decision. She could see that I was dead serious, but I also made it clear that I would *not* make the move without her approval. She also understood that she would be a working partner. I painted a realistic picture, glossing over nothing. She realized that all "perks" would be forfeited and that we might have to subsist on pancakes and cheap hamburger for an indefinite period. She could *also* see that I deeply longed for the independence and challenge the move would provide. Before Anne could reply, Eleanor came in to announce that she could no longer keep Jane occupied. We promptly tabled the conversation and hoped that Jane would go to sleep early. The ball playing with Eleanor apparently tired her out. It wasn't long before she was fast asleep. Anne, Eleanor and I then gathered around the dining room table as I tried to put my plans before them in a positive light. As I had hoped—and rather expected—as soon as Anne overcame her initial shock and fear, she smiled warmly and said, "I have to admit that it's scary—but I trust your judgment and have faith in you, Frank. I know it's what you *really* want to do so—let's go for it!" El chimed in, "You'll make a good team. I'll be praying for you."

After the teary hugs and kisses, we discussed the next steps in this dramatic turning point in our lives. El had a job as a sales clerk in a clothing store, so Anne would have to get Jane after school each day. Applications and approval for business licenses—state and local—would have to be obtained. A low-rent office would be required. Furniture, telephones—the list grew at an alarming pace. Phil had revealed that he had started "on a shoestring," but was making a modest profit in just a few months. I kept reminding myself that there was no reason that I couldn't follow the same pattern. I certainly had the "shoestring" part down pat. The minor profit from the sale of our Madison home would have to be tapped; cashing in Anne's insurance policy would bring five hundred dollars. These, plus hard work and God's good grace would simply *have* to get our desired result. Failure was not an option. All of these preparatory measures would have to be taken *before* I dropped the bombshell in Bill's lap. I had seen people give a two-week notice of quitting, and then be ushered out the front gate by a security officer that very day. There was a "You're either 100% with us or you're against us—You're out of here!" policy. Bill used it on several occasions. I didn't want it to happen to me.

Before making application to the Employment Agency Board in Sacramento, approval of the business location was required; this was required for a city license also. Where to go? By chance (is there such a thing?) Anne saw a "space for rent" sign in the window of a small freestanding building. The location was excellent. It was only a half block off the main street in the heart of Covina. The building was approximately fourteen feet wide and forty feet deep and had large windows facing the street. Below the sign in the window was a note: "See Covina Awning and Shade manager inside." Hoping against hope, Anne walked in. She could see that the front half of the building was empty and comprised the available space. Having heard the door open, the landlord stepped in from the back room and greeted Anne warmly; his wife immediately joined him. "Hi! I'm Al Duncan and this is my wife, Hazel. You're here about the office space?" Al was a "blunt, candid, slap-on-the-back" sort of fellow who bore a striking resemblance to Mr. Wilson of the "Dennis the Menace" cartoon. The bulbous nose, the pudginess; the thinning hair. He smoked a cigar instead of a pipe, however. Hazel too was on the stocky side—probably in her sixties, trying vainly to hang onto youth through an excess of eye makeup.

"Hazel and I assemble and repair blinds, shades, awnings—stuff like that—in the back half. What kind of business you in?" "None, *yet*." Anne then added with alacrity, "But my husband and I intend to open an employment agency soon!" Although it was only mid-afternoon, Al's glazed eyes and a distinct odor of alcohol made it obvious to Anne that he was more than just a social drinker. Hazel sensed Anne's concern. "Why don't you have your husband come back with you and see what he thinks? If it's what you're both looking for, we'll talk about a fair rental agreement. How's that sound?" With restrained and diluted enthusiasm, Anne replied, "Great. I'll talk to him tonight." As she left the building, she paused on the walkway in front, turned for another look at it and murmured, "Lord, guide us!"

When Anne told me of her discovery, I discerned her expected fervor to be more temperate. She confessed, "There could be a problem." "I suspected as much. What is it?" She haltingly told of her suspicion that Al was an alcoholic. Reluctant to see such a vital part of our dream slip away, I said cheerfully, "Maybe it's not as serious as it seems. The location and size sound absolutely *perfect* for our *very* small business."

Because of my rather late return from work—and because I wanted to observe Al in the afternoon, we made an appointment for three o'clock Saturday. Our friend, Betty Jo agreed to have Jane over during our absence.

Even before entering the building, I knew in my heart that this *had* to be the place where we would launch a new life and enter a new world of independence. Al would have to be a *reeeeeally* bad dude or ask an outrageous rent before I would miss *this* opportunity.

Anne was right about Al being a drinker, but he and Hazel were so friendly, amiable and jolly that I expected their coziness to be a cover for an exorbitant rental agreement. To our everlasting joy and surprise, the terms were more than acceptable. They even offered to answer our phone if we were both out when it rang. "There's always *some* drawback to be expected." I thought as we signed the rental agreement. Even after we learned "the bottle" played an important role in their otherwise sterile lives, it became apparent that they conducted their business with propriety. Nor was either of them abusive or obnoxious. Al *was* often loud and boisterous, but it was a small price to pay for his providing us with the cornerstone to what we hoped would be a rewarding new life.

***

The first question on the application for an agency license stumped me. "Name of proposed agency." I knew that Phil's agency was called "Crane Employment Agency," but hadn't given a thought to naming ours. "Balensiefer" was obviously out. The name had to be short and easily understood on the telephone as well as in print. People invariably butchered our name. Everything from Balenscooper to Blasenfelder. What to do? Then it occurred to me. Bob Finucane, my college chum, roommate and lifelong friend, had a nickname in the service that was of unrecalled origin; it was "R.C. Dobbs." Perfect! We would call our business "Dobbs Personnel Agency." Anne immediately agreed, adding, "I'm sure Bob will be proud to hear that." He was, indeed.

My carefully scripted speech announcing my termination became ashes in my already dry mouth. I started with, "Bill, I have something that I hate to tell you." "You're leaving us, right?" His usual smile/frown had more emphasis on "frown." "This isn't easy for me, Bill. I feel like a heel, but I've decided to start my own employment agency." "I knew something pretty heavy's been on your mind. I'm disappointed, to say the least. We had big plans for you, Frank, but you have to do what you have to do. Tell me about it."

When I finished my rather animated description of my plans, Bill's demeanor had decidedly softened. In fact, as I was about to leave, through his frowning smile and firm handshake, he spoke huskily, "I wish you nothing but the best, Frank."

Of course, the transition took time. I had to indoctrinate my replacement, who was brought in from another plant. And, as I said my goodbyes to those with whom I had worked, the lump in my throat felt like a permanent fixture. But the cord was finally cut. Nor would I miss the dreaded commute to Los Angeles.

A moment etched in our memory is when Anne and I watched the final touches of the sign being completed on the front door of our new office. In eight-inch gold leaf letters it read simply, "Dobbs Personnel Agency."

Anne looked up at me and wistfully asked, "Shouldn't we have "W.P.T.*" inscribed somewhere?" "Works for me," I replied with a wry smile. With that we opened the door to a fruitful and rewarding new life. It was frightening, but we remembered the sage adage, "If you try, you RISK failure. If you don't try, you GUARANTEE it."

---

*We'll pull through.

COUNTRY ROAD

We had established good solid friendships and enjoyed our cozy little home in Covina. Our business had been relatively successful despite the disillusioning fact that Oscar Mayer would *not* let us provide job applicants for their openings. We knew that many job openings existed, but we also knew of Oscar's attitude toward anyone who had the effrontery and disloyalty to quit the company. If you left Oscar Mayer—voluntarily or otherwise—you were blacklisted. You were anathema. I didn't blame the personnel manager: dealing with a "traitor" like me would put his job I jeopardy. Some of Oscar Mayer's management was just full of baloney. It would feel good to develop my own business without their help.

Two words that served us well in establishing our business were *faith* and *perseverance*. Gaining a foothold in a strange business community required shoe-leather and a convincing telephone technique. Knocking on factory office doors and calling personnel managers eventually produced favorable results. We developed job openings, advertised for applicants and found that we enjoyed being "matchmakers." In a few short months of concerted effort, we began to realize a slight profit. Before long, we added an employee and were off and running. Within three years we had moved to a larger office and added two more employment counselors.

Most of us experience what we might call "turning points" in our lives—occasions that have dramatic effects on our future. Our "turning points" were frequent and profound. Starting our own business had been one of the most wrenching and life-altering events, but, near the end of our seventh year in Covina, we were about to make another pivotal move.

Jane had expressed a love for horses ever since she began to walk and talk. "I wish I had a horse," was a continual refrain from her. My standard response was, "Maybe someday, honey." I brushed it off as pie-in-the-sky for a while until one Sunday as I was scanning the newspaper a bold advertisement grabbed me by the throat and wouldn't let go. It read, "HORSE LOVERS—THIS IF FOR YOU! BRIDLEWOOD of ALTA LOMA offers RANCHETTES." I showed the ad to Anne and said, "Want to take a run up there?" Making sure that Jane couldn't hear, she continued, "Don't let Jane know. Let's go tomorrow while she's in school. No need to get her hopes up 'til we look into it—but it *does* sound ideal."

By this time, we had trained employees who could run the business during our short absences, so we were able to leave for Alta Loma the next morning. We found it to be only a thirty to forty minute drive to Bridlewood. The drive became more exciting and appealing the farther we got from Covina. Pepper trees, eucalyptus, liquid amber, and sagebrush lined our path as we climbed steeply to the two thousand foot level. We both felt very much at home in the rugged, rural atmosphere. Approaching the sales office, we noticed a row of rather plain, ranch-style homes. As advertised, the area was clearly planned for equestrian use. Each house had a large corral space, abutting an extensive bridal trail. The developer had generously provided each house with a tiny curbside tree. Landscaping was limited to "landscraping." Most rocks and debris had been scraped away from each lot. The soil was somewhat like a moraine, comprised of about eighty percent rock. Vegetation was sparse. These negative features did nothing to diminish our approval. They were merely challenges that we could conquer—later. Besides, a friend of ours was a land-scape designer and owned a nursery in Covina. The potential was obvious and the price was right, so we felt that the whole situation was providential.

The salesman who spoke to us in the model home had little selling to do. He did try, nonetheless. In doing so, he made a statement that later proved to be utterly unfounded. Knowing our interest in a rural atmosphere, he asserted that no houses would be built above us because the land belonged to "God and the government."

We had often heard the cliché, "Decide in haste; repent at leisure" so we told the salesman we would "sleep on it" and give him our decision soon. *Sleep* on it? Hardly! We tossed and turned and whispered our mutual thoughts much of that night. Nor had it been easy to conceal our excitement from Jane.

When dawn finally dragged its way out of the clinging darkness, I turned to Anne and merely asked, "Well?" "Let's do it! Let's be there when their doors open. I hope they're not all *sold*!" Her words were a mixture of joy and anxiety. "Glad we didn't let Jane in on it. It's not definite 'til we sign the final papers and we have to get loan approval, you know," I added with my own degree of concern.

Confident of our return, Tom—the salesman—had our papers ready to sign, contingent upon loan approval, of course. As we dealt with the myriad documents, there was a knock on the door and a strikingly attractive, blue-eyed blond entered the room. With apologies and some diffidence, she asked Tom for the keys to the house that she and her husband had just purchased. Beaming, Tom nearly stumbled over his own feet as he arose and, flustered, fumbled for the keys. "Sure, Mrs. Hearl. They're here somewhere." He stared like a lovesick schoolboy as she took the keys, softly closed the door and left. I finally had to say, "Uh—Mr. Nugent, you were saying...?" "Oh! Yeah—where were we?" he stammered.

Upon completing the last document, Anne asked about Mrs. Hearl. Tom Nugent told us that her name was Carla; her husband's name was Larry, but was called "Bud;" that they had a daughter, Robin, about Jane's age; a son, Scott, about nine or ten, and that their house was about five lots east of ours. "Jane will be happy to hear about Robin. Who knows? We might all become friends," Anne spoke with alacrity.

When Jane's last class ended, we were there to give her the good news. "What have you been wanting for a long time, Jane?" Anne asked. "A horse, of course, but I know..." Then, seeing our glowing smiles, she gasped, "You don't mean..." "Yes, honey, you're finally going to get your horse." We then explained about our move to Alta Loma. At that point, it's doubtful that she really cared about the new house. She was having visions of herself astride her *own* horse. Now all we had to do was move to our new house, build a barn, erect a corral fence, and find a gentle horse—in that order. The fun/work was about to begin.

IF I WERE A CARPENTER

M oving from one residence to another was not a new experience for us. But, going from a semi-tropical setting to a rugged half-acre of sand, gravel and rock presented challenges unlike those of our previous moves.

The home itself was new and met all basic requirements—no frills—just the usual necessities. Nevertheless, we were thrilled to envision the possibilities for the property. We gave priority to the building of a corral. Next would be the constructing of a barn—small, but large enough for a stall on one half and tack room on the other. These completed, we would start our search for a suitable horse. The landscaping; the patios—front and rear; the room addition and other modifications would have to wait. Horse-related projects headed my agenda. Anne was busy "setting up housekeeping" during my frequent forays to the lumberyard.

I soon learned that I was the typical "greenhorn ten-derfoot." It came as quite a shock when I discovered the harsh reality of post-hole digging in mountain-slope soil. Beneath a thin, deceptive layer of topsoil lies at least eighty percent stone and boulder. Strategically placed bits of dynamite were the only solution that occurred to me. But then the thought of lost fingers and who knows what else killed that idea. A pickaxe and a six-foot pry bar would have to do. Something else I should have known was the need to fill each large hole with concrete to secure the post.

Some of the boulders I encountered while trying to dig holes were so large that I had to hire a man who had a skip-loader. We had him take the three largest ones and place them near the entrance to our driveway. We've never regretted that small investment. They have become part of our identity. Giving directions to our house was made easier. "We're the place with the three boulders."

Barn construction was another interesting challenge. My knowledge of carpentry and construction was confined to that which I gained from designing and assembling a small rocking horse for then three-year-old Jane. It soon became eminently clear that such experience does *not* qualify one to design, construct and erect a *building*.

One of the most profound pronouncements ever uttered is, "Attitude is everything," yet I found "every-thing" to be a bit strong. I had the right attitude but found that something more was required. A good attitude won't build a barn. Oh, I *did* have the basics; a hammer; nails; a saw; a tape measure and a ladder. I hadn't thought of a level; t-square; metal joist connectors and a few other construction needs. I had sketched out a plan and ordered the lumber, rolls of roofing and both red and white barn paint. My little barn was to be a thing of beauty—a stall and tack room worthy of a Seabiscuit or a Seattle Slew.

I decided not to lay a concrete floor, thinking that this would be unfair to the poor horse. *Big mistake.* Talk about misplaced compassion! (I reflected upon this later, as I tried vainly to separate the manure from the "Alta Loma soil.") No, constructing my bucolic Taj Mahal was not the piece of cake I had envisioned.

We were ecstatic as we watched the lumbering, heavily laden delivery truck thread its way through the narrow bridle path toward our corral. But, as we saw the pile upon pile of 2x4s, 2x6s, 4'x8'plywood sheets, roofing, etc. dumped in a heap on the ground, it was a scary thing. We felt overwhelmed and somewhat dysfunctional.

Anne spoke with arms akimbo. "Well, cowboy, you wanted a barn. Got any idea where to begin?" "Welllll," I drawled, "I reckon we'd better---Whoa! What was that?!" A deafening thunderclap fairly shook the timber as bullet-like raindrops began their ballet on the boards. "We have paint drop cloths in the house. Let's get them, *now*!" Feet pounding mud, we rushed to retrieve the drop cloths and soon had most of the wood covered. Having lived in the Southern California for over seven years, we *never* saw rain in September, but of course *this* year...!

Once in the house, we looked out at the downpour. I creased my brow, stroked my chin and pondered, "How 'bout we start with the roof?" I braced for the hit that I knew would come. "*Very* funny!" Then in mock exasperation, she hit my shoulder and began pummeling me with soft blows as I bobbed and weaved. We were soon exhausted but laughing heartily.

The rain stopped during the night, but left puddles of mud and didn't spare the partially exposed wood. We hastily wiped the dampness from the wood (the wind had blown some of the drop cloth off). Water could cause warping—at least, we knew *that* much.

With no concrete for a foundation, it became painfully clear that post-holes would have to be dug for the corner posts. Back to the pickaxe and pry bar and more sore muscles. "Where are the Amish when we need them?" I moaned as I recalled scenes of the "barn raising" by a cheerful group of black-hatted, bearded workers. Anne, my willing and able factotum, kept me supplied with food and drink; gave me nails; held the ladder and performed a broad variety of "go-fer" functions.

After several days of hard labor and much "trial and error," we were ready to add the roof to the framework. I had no idea how heavy a sheet of 4'x8' x1/2" plywood could be. It took every ounce of my strength to push, pull and shove each of many sheets to lay on the rafters. Nor was that the end of it. Next came rolls of tarpaper, roofing, adhesive and nails. With Anne's help and encouragement ("Can I help?" "You can do it!" "Just a few more…") we finished the roof and were ready to nail the siding to the frame. After the agony of roofing, the rest of the construction was a breeze. As I put the final screw in the door hinge, I heaved a heavy sigh, "I hope we get an appreciative horse!"

Having completed the painting by the end of the next day, we were rewarded by the glow of an autumn sunset, giving the red barn and white trim a radiant sheen.

We literally *fell* into bed that night. I moaned, "My aching muscles tell me I don't belong in the construction business." "Amen to that," sighed Anne.

BUTTONS AND BOWS

Jane was getting impatient—and who could blame her? It had taken several weeks to erect the corral and construct the barn. Despite our explaining that it would take time, she thought that we would *surely* get a horse within a few days of our move-in. A week is seven days to an adult, but often a month to a child—especially when waiting for an exciting event. And this was, indeed, to be an exceptionally thrilling occasion for Jane—and to us, to a lesser extent.

We had subscribed to the local newspaper and regularly scanned the "Horses for Sale" column. Most of the ads had some feature that eliminated the horse from our consideration. We called and visited the ones that sounded like possibilities, but none seemed quite right. We began to wonder whether we would *ever* find one that would be suitable for an inexperienced rider like Jane.

The day finally came when we tried out a gentle old bay gelding. Jane mounted "Charlie" with ease, then after only a few steps, gleefully announced, "I want Charlie!" The search was over. We were delighted, to say the least—and the price was right. Good thing it was because the tack—something we hadn't considered—was more costly than the horse! When Charlie's former owner delivered him to our corral, he drawled, "Y'all got tack, aintcha?" Somewhat embarrassed at my ignorance, I mumbled, "Well, we do have a tack-*room*—ha ha—but truth is, we don't." He smiled knowingly, "I think I have what you need in my trailer." He then proceeded to lay out a western saddle, a bridle, a halter and a training bit. He topped it off with a lead-rope, saying, "That lil package oughta do it." With some anxiety I asked, "How much?" "Welllll—they's a lotta gear there, but I'll make you a deal." I don't recall the actual amount he quoted, but I *do* remember that we were shocked when we heard it. I would warn anyone who considers buying a horse, "Tack ain't cheap!" Nor are feed, veterinarian bills, riding habits and riding lessons.

Oh, yes—riding lessons. Another surprise. Someone had recommended a local training school, so we took Jane to apply the day after getting Charlie. She quickly learned that there was *much* more to properly riding a horse than mounting, moving ahead and dismounting. To add to the ever-expanding list of needs, we found that an *English* saddle and a complete outfit (jacket, English riding boots, jodhpurs, velour riding cap, silk blouse, and ascot) was required. It was an expensive arrangement, but well worth it—especially when we saw the look on Jane's face when she won her first blue ribbon in gymkhana. She did *not*, however, win it with Charlie.

Charlie was very easygoing, gentle and good for a beginner or a flat trail, but he was *not* a show horse—and a show horse with spirit was required to achieve ribbon-winning performance in the ring. At the embarrassingly pointed "suggestion" of the trainer, we began our search once again.

Now that we were more experienced, it took less time to find a worthy show horse. Following up on an ad, we were more than pleased to find the advertised horse to be truly a thing of beauty. It was a half Arabian and half Thoroughbred gelding. A forehead star and white fetlocks embellished its sleek sorrel hide. Something in its huge blue eyes gave me an uneasy feeling, but it didn't bother Jane. She thought he was not only a fine specimen of a horse but cute as a button. In fact, she ignored his registered name and called him "Buttons." In my opinion—and Anne's—"Dynamite" would have been more appropriate. Initially, his explosive temperament could only be soothed by Jane. He was extremely sensitive and easily excited, but became more docile with Jane. He *did*, however, throw her one day during practice in our training ring. Fortunately, she was wearing a protective helmet. Eleanor had been watching, and when she saw Jane hit the ground, she ran to her, struck Buttons mightily with a broom and shouted, "Get away, you mean beast! Don't you hurt my granddaughter!" Still lying on the ground, dazed, Jane squeaked, "Don't hurt him, Grandma. I'll be all right." Anne and I had been away but returned shortly after the incident. Under Jane's protest, we took her to the hospital and found that she had suffered a mild concussion. There was not permanent damage. Both Anne and her mother refused to mount the horse thereafter.

Several of us horse owners got together and decided to start a riding club in the large field below our property. We called it simply the "Alta Loma Riding Club." We set up a gigantic ring, high overhead lights, bleachers and a refreshment stand. The club was so popular that we eventually hosted statewide horse shows, awarding ribbons to the winning competitors. After considerable training, Jane and Buttons were able to win in competition with more experienced riders.

Many of the adults in our group rode their sons' and daughters' horses for pleasure. It was still wide-open country with much to explore, so I was determined to conquer Buttons' feistiness and ride with the others. It took time, patience and a few bruises, but I eventually made a deal with the horse: If he would yield a certain degree of control to me, he would be spared the pain of my spurs and riding crop. The arrangement worked rather well, although I must admit to hanging onto the pommel of the western saddle on more than one occasion. There is no pommel on an English saddle, of course, but this was not a problem for Jane. She didn't need one.

Some time after forming the riding club (which, after forty years, is still active), several of us recognized a need for a posse and an equestrian search and rescue team. The local sheriff's department was delighted. We formed a posse and were officially deputized. We had gun permits, badges and a dress code. The posse was involved in several harrowing rescues—mostly because of inexperienced hikers who had little respect for—or even awareness of—the danger and treachery of our mountains. To reach a rendezvous point, a horse-trailer was often needed. I had none, so I shared one with another deputy. "Trailering" Buttons was like trying to single-handedly corral a herd of wild mustangs. We knew he hated confinement, but the mere sight of a horse-trailer sent him into an equine version of a panic attack. We tried everything from gentle coaxing to whippings. The only method that worked was the use of thick straps on his hindquarters and a makeshift wench; this, in effect, *shoved* him in, despite his spirited protests.

At my first attempt to trailer Buttons, his eyes bulged with raw fear. I even wondered, "Do horses get claustrophobia? And do they imagine a trailer is only for delivering them to a glue factory?" Whatever the reason, Buttons would have none of it. I took considerable ribbing from my partner when he saw me trying the power of suggestion by slowly ascending the ramp on all fours in front of the horse. I kept saying, "See, Buttons, it's easy. There's nothing to it. C'mon up." Instead of yielding to my gentle tug on the lead-rope, he reared back, pawed the air and whinnied as if to say, "No *way*! You're not getting *me* in that trap!" So much for animal psychology!

※

Jane and I saw to it that the horse got daily exercise—a good thing for all concerned. We had learned that many horses become "barn sour" through inactivity. They become lazy and slow, adding credence to the old saw, "If you don't use, you lose it."

In a few short years, however, Jane's enthusiasm for riding began to flag. Nor did she enjoy the work that was required for the care and feeding of the horse. Her attention became focused on *automobiles* and *boys*—not necessarily in that order. I, too, was devoting an increasing amount of time to promoting our business and less time to riding. It no longer made any sense to prolong the inevitable. Buttons would have to be sold. Jane was reluctant and saddened when I told her, but had to agree that it wasn't even fair to Buttons who loved to run flat out at top speed. He wasn't getting the attention or exercise he needed.

An Arabian show-horse was (and is) a sought-after prize, so we had little trouble in finding a buyer. That was the easy part. Finding a buyer who could *control* the horse was a major problem. By this time, Buttons had finally learned that a trailer did *not* represent a one-way trip to the glue factory, so we had little trouble delivering him to the first family that agreed to buy him. They could see that he was a "spirited" animal, but passed off his skittishness to being unfamiliar with the new owner. Only a few hours after our delivery, however, we received a phone call from the buyer. "Sir—you're gonna hafta come and get this horse. He's a wild one. He tried to buck each one of us off!" We had accepted a check, but, of course, hadn't had time to cash it, so we returned it to the disappointed (and somewhat angered) family. I apologized. "I'm terribly sorry. He's been just fine with us." When this same scenario presented itself a second and a *third* time, we were about to conclude that no one but Jane or I could handle the unruly beast. When we sold it the *fourth* time, we made it very clear that the horse was hard to handle, but the prospective buyer took that as a personal challenge. "Hey, I used to bust broncos. I can whip him into shape." It was late in the day and the banks were closed, so I accepted the man's check. The next morning, however, I was the first person to enter the bank as it opened. I sighed with relief as I pocketed the cash and headed for the office. No sooner had I reached my desk than I got a frightened call from Anne. "Frank, Mr. Edgars just called. He sounded upset and wants you to call him right away!" I had not given my work number, of course. "Not again!" I agonized. "Well, this one's not getting his money back. He was warned." I took a few deep breaths, convinced myself that I was in control—that I would *not* return the money, and then dialed the number.

Predictably, the man wanted me to come and get the horse and to return his money. After some emotional haggling, I finally agreed to give him the saddles (which I had hoped to sell separately). I closed the conversation with, "With your bronc-busting experience, Mr. Edgars, you'll have Buttons "whipped into shape" in *no* time," and cradled the receiver.

I wasn't really surprised when it was *Mrs.* Edgars who came for the saddles. I *was* surprised when she called us at home one evening about two weeks later. "Jed was too embarrassed to call you, but I just had to let you know that our thirteen-year-old, Sarah, is doing just *great* with Buttons. It's like they were made for each other!"

Maybe there *is* something to animal psychology—"Transference," perhaps? Whatever it was, it pleased Jane to know that Buttons was happy again—Of course, so were we.

SUNRISE-SUNSET

*S*hortly after receiving her high school diploma, Jane married an arrogant, longhaired wild young man from New York—a fellow she met through a mutual friend. After a brief courtship, they were married—despite our vigorous expressions of disapproval.

Jane's husband, Eddie, was irrationally jealous, possessive and insecure. Shortly after their marriage, he began to imagine that Jane was being untrue to him. So violent was his temper that, in a fit of unwarranted anger, during a neighborhood party, he grabbed a knife and stabbed her—again and again—a total of *twenty-five* times. He shouted, "If I can't have you, nobody can!" Someone observed the attempted murder, pulled Eddie away and rushed Jane to a nearby hospital. Anne and I were visiting friends—about twenty miles from the hospital. A friend of Jane's—who was at the party—knew this and called to alert us. We rushed frantically to the emergency ward and found

Jane barely alive. The attending physician said that, had five minutes more elapsed before her entering the hospital, they could not have saved her.

By a baffling twist of "justice," Eddie was held in a prison but a few days. He was then ordered to "get treatment for anger management!" He went to a local college psychologist for several sessions and that satisfied the spineless judge. Meanwhile, we nursed Jane through her long and painful recovery. He chest, lungs, hands and other areas of her body had received multiple stab wounds.

We had often heard of battered women forgiving their cruel husbands and returning to them (for more punishment). We never imagined that Jane would succumb to the remorseful pleas of her truculent and devious husband. We quickly learned how futile are objective, honest words of warning to a woman in love. She decided to go back to him. Reason, logic and common sense were eschewed with comments such as, "Oh, I *know* how sorry he is. He'll never do it again. He's a changed man."

To our pleasant surprise, this was partly true. He did not physically abuse her thereafter, but his incessant verbal abuse made her life miserable. Nevertheless, determined to hold the marriage together, she stayed with him for several years. Having two lovely daughters during this period made her life more bearable. She now had someone besides her parents with whom she could share love and affection.

Two years after the birth of her second daughter, Erin, Jane's life was again devastated by a painful divorce. This trauma, added to the ravaging effects of Post Traumatic Stress Disorder, rendered her incapable of keeping a job. Jane could not support her children and her (former) husband refused to care for them. Nor would the children live with him (and his "live-in") anyway. He would actually beat them with a leather belt and demean them mercilessly. Eventually, Anne and I became their legal guardians. The resulting stress on all of us—Anne and myself, Jane, Erin, Christina and yes, even Eleanor, was dreadful. I say "even" Eleanor because she had been living in her own apartment for quite some time, and did not experience the daily problems we faced.

The strain of the divorce, combined with her cease-less post-traumatic stress, finally drove Jane to the breaking point. Deep, severe and lasting depression rendered her incapable of living a normal, productive life. Psychotherapy and anti-depressant medication were of some help, but to this day we are uncertain of how far she has traveled on the road to recovery. We can only hope and pray that she is past the half-way point. Her behavior is too inconsistent for us to make an accurate evaluation. She does have a good relationship with her daughters—as she would with her grandmother, were Eleanor alive. (Eleanor had endured years of the effects of Alzheimer's Disease before passing away at ninety-six).

CODA

The corral is now home to a lemon tree, a grape-fruit tree, a pepper tree, and olive tree and a large pine. The barn has become a repository for everything from holiday decorations to furniture. The riding ring holds a small motor home—one that gets even more exercise than we gave Buttons.

Anne and I are retired; Erin is out of high school and seeking a career; Christina is engaged and employed; Jane is making a valiant effort to pull herself up and out of the pit so deeply hollowed out by depression. Clearly, there *is* hope and much for which to be thankful.

Having long since passed the September of my years, I find myself reflecting upon the events and conditions that have coalesced to form the matrix for my destiny. These eight decades of experience have helped provide knowledge of some of the ingredients for a fulfilling, rewarding life. In part, they are:

- A positive attitude, blended with a mature acceptance of unwanted conditions that are beyond our control.
- Good health of both mind and body—an *acquired* condition for most people. Rarely is this achieved without concerted effort and self-discipline.
- There is considerable wisdom in the admonition to "carpe diem."
- A consuming interest in *something*—anything, from ant farms to zithers.
- Enthusiasm—such an appropriate word! Its stem is Latin, "enthusiasmus," literally, "God in us."

Having the correct ingredients does not, however, produce the final product. What then is the sine qua non, after all is said and done? Curiously, the defining phrase is found in a song (why are you not surprised?) so well sung by the late Nat King Cole:

*The greatest thing
you'll ever learn
is just to love
and be loved in return.*

ABOUT THE AUTHOR

FRANK BALENSIEFER is an eclectic author of many publications. Further credentials include over forty years experience in the field of Human Resources.

After attending Purdue University, Wabash College and Syracuse University he received a degree in Psychology from Colorado College.

In addition to The Job Search Game, Winds and Strings and Silver Wings and a comprehensive anthology, he numbers short stories, articles and essays among his literary achievements. His current endeavor is a novel of the Adventure, Intrigue and Romance genre. Don't miss it!

Printed in the United States
58592LVS00001B/1-30